5/01

# Monstruary

# Monstruary

by

# JULIÁN RÍOS

*Translated by Edith Grossman*

ALFRED A. KNOPF ❧ NEW YORK 2001

THIS IS A BORZOI BOOK
PUBLISHED BY ALFRED A. KNOPF

www.aaknopf.com

Originally published in Spain as *Monstruario* by Seix Barral,
Barcelona, in 1999. Copyright © 1999 by Julián Ríos.
Copyright © 1999 by Editorial Seix Barral, S. A.

Knopf, Borzoi Books, and the colophon are registered
trademarks of Random House, Inc.

Library of Congress Cataloging-in-Publication Data
Ríos, Julián.
[Monstruary. English]
Monstruario / by Julián Ríos ; translated by Edith Grossman.
p.   cm.
ISBN 0-375-40823-1 (hc : alk. paper)
I. Grossman, Edith.    II. Title.
PQ6668.I576 M6613 2001
863'.64—dc21          00-040547

Manufactured in the United States of America
First American Edition

# Contents

# Monstruary

Now I don't know if I'm the Mummy or the Invisible Man, said Mons with some difficulty through his bandages, and we laughed, relieved to suppose that along with his good humor he had also recovered his reason. Klaus and I would be the usual monsters again—Klaus the Zombie and Emil the Old Satyr—unless we became the Stick Man and the Abominable Snowman we had been long ago, in the good old London days, and Double Uwe continued his hic-hic-hiccuping, shaking his huge body of a Pantagruelian ogre who devours lines of artists, which is how Mons had painted him. And the three of us, strategically placed at the foot and both flanks of his bed, as if to cut off an impossible escape, helped him to reconstruct the enigma—never more aptly called a hard nut to crack—of his final days and nights in Berlin. Right we are if we think we are? Mons nodded or shook his bandaged head—it was still especially difficult for him to speak—or raised a hand slightly (his hands were bandaged as well) when he couldn't make us understand. Sometimes he opened his eyes wide—two coals, edged in red—through the slits in the bandages. Three days after the accident he was still confused—and agitated at times—by the feeling that the most broken part of him was his memory. He recalled a series of images, disconcerting and disconnected, as if they had come from his own *Mon-*

*struary*. Or from the awful intermittent delirium of the past few hours in which we were capriciously embroiled though we could make out only occasional words and names. Or believed we understood those gabbled sounds.

What's he saying now? But who's he calling? Double Uwe kept repeating.

Mélusine, Dr. Koppel deciphered with some satisfaction; but only I, the eminent biographer, as Mons mockingly calls me at times, could know that Mélusine was not a product of the painter's imagination—did not come from the gallery of monsters in *Monstruary* but from his own past: one of the ladies from his heroic days. A French student of fine arts and waitress in London. Her name was Armelle, but Mons changed it to Mélusine when she began to disappear mysteriously on Saturdays. Until he discovered that when she went out early on Saturdays, hiding behind dark glasses and carrying a large bag over her shoulder, she was going not to play tennis with a girlfriend but to perform a really high-powered striptease at various Soho clubs in order to pay the rent for the room they shared behind the Portobello Road. At that time Mons was doing portraits in the streets. He would acknowledge his ingratitude when he left her almost overnight after a commission, or rather a stroke of good fortune, allowed him to make the trip to New York he had wanted for so long. Mélusine, Dr. Koppel explained to us, was a fairy who had married a count of Poitiers. She would not permit anyone, not even her husband, to see her on Saturdays, because on that day her beautiful legs were transformed into a serpent's tail. *Mélusine's Striptease* is the title of the painting in which a naked Armelle holds up a stocking that looks like a snakeskin.

The spider, Mons seemed to mumble, and I was afraid Dr. Koppel would tell us the story of Arachne. The spider woman? I believe Mons was referring to his stepsister, Ara, who as a child frequently writhed in a net hammock. And was a ballerina. Then I recalled the nude portrait of the slender brunette with straight hair, almond eyes, and a long Modiglianiesque neck, seated on a bench of light wood, her head leaning against her left shoulder, her open hands resting beside her thighs, and a round black hairy spider on her pubis. Miss Tarantula, Mons explained to me. She had worked as a masseuse in a sauna on Wardour Street in the late sixties, and her tattoo was not the least of her charms. Dr. Koppel continued listening, leaning over the mask of bandages.

When I looked at Dr. Koppel, with his bare skull, convex forehead, and deep purplish circles under his eyes, what I really saw was the portrait Mons had recently painted of him in a white coat, bending over a crystal ball in which his almost spherical, all-knowing head was reflected. The psychiatrist reads the future or his own mind? I had asked Mons, who only shrugged and raised his eyebrows.

Mons mumbled again, or moaned, and turned his head toward the window when the doctor asked if he wanted something. To leave? Through the high window you could see the lacy silhouettes of trees like a second dark curtain blown by the wind. As night fell he began to rave again, though he was less agitated than yesterday. Just half an hour earlier the abrupt entrance of a nurse with bright red hair— yes, like a sudden flame—pulled Mons back to his earlier figurations and transfigurations. "Vampire!" is what he said, and he struggled in his bed until the nurse, leaning over him, managed to inject the sedative. We could not suspect that Mons at that moment was seeing—or seeing again in the red blaze—the woman sitting next to a brazier, spreading her thick hair, like threads of blood, over the head and shoulders of the disconsolate man who has taken refuge in her arms and sobs with his face against her breast while she seems to kiss and cradle him but in reality bites the nape of his neck and sucks his blood until he is drained dry. At least that is what Mons claimed on the freezing night in late November when we saw, in an empty lot near Checkpoint Charlie, the girl with hair dyed flaming red who was tilting back a bottle with some truck drivers beside a fire in a steel drum until at last she passed out or began to cry on the shoulder of the youngest one, who seemed as drunk as she was. Or as we were. And she is she is—Mons asserted a little later in a gloomy Kreuzberg café appropriately called Malheur, his tongue stumbling as it usually does when he begins his over-wrought skald's epic sagas—she is the image of Petra, his Petrushka, a German girl who was half Polish and half Russian and a chameleon of every stripe—Wigged-out Wig, he called her, though her hair, regularly dyed in streaks of gaudy colors, was her own—who, in addition to painting still lifes of bottles like Morandi and serving drinks, posed as a model and reminded him of his original model, the genuine Crackpot Pole, Eva "Lalka," the Doll, in Polish, that's what she called herself, her artistic name, his muse for a few mad months in London. Between striding down fashion runways and posing for photographs, Eva Lalka still found time to be a Sunday artist, a minimalist photographer, dashing here and there like a squirrel, though in the middle of a session she could suddenly freeze or sink into a lethargy only to revive a short while later, stretching her body to even greater lengths and opening her hollow dark eyes very wide, like the time Mons found her in her darkroom, which was crisscrossed with ropes in a kind of net or strange spider's web. And she appeared caught in the arms of a muscular black model. In order to evoke that multiple Eva who had vanished years before, the chameleonesque German girl was his dark-haired, wasp-waisted *La signorina Spalanzani* with one hand on her pubis, like Manet's Olympia; and his platinum blond *Future Eve*, a mechanical mannequin, burnished and compact like some of Léger's tubular figures; and his horrific *Kokoschka's Doll*, a redhead or rather a brunette with hair half-dyed by recently spilled red wine, or perhaps blood; and then she disappeared from Berlin without a trace. Wasn't she the girl in the phosphorescent wig waiting for clients in a car parked in the wasteland of Potsdamer Platz that snowy night? And he saw her again after almost three months, he was certain—last Thursday, another night of too much drinking, in the artists' commune or rather the monster factory that occupies an entire, entirely decrepit six- or seven-story building in Prenzlauer Berg near the elevated railroad on Dimitroffstrasse, maybe Knaackstrasse. Mons clearly remembers the grimy facade covered with graffiti and slogans, its crumbling rectangular balconies, some windows boarded up and many with broken glass. Poking through a window on the fourth or fifth floor was an old filthy mop or messy Medusa or rotting head of a gorgon on a pike. And from the next window hung a sheet with the name of the commune or nest of new nihilists, in huge black letters: NIFLHEIM.

Going home means dying a little, Klaus told Mons,

pointing at the sheet, and the two pale punks guarding the entrance indicated their approval by showing their fangs. Almost as long, said Mons, as those of the hairy wolfhound growling a greeting as he and Klaus crossed the first interior courtyard of that house of monsters, that's what Mons called it, in the company or custody of the strange Nosferatu in strict mourning and the greatcoated giant with the square head and the movements of an automaton whom we had met in the subterranean bar on Oranienstrasse almost at the end of the night that would be all-monsters' night and began appropriately enough in the studio of Mons, who had fallen asleep over his latest productions.

Victor? Victor . . . I pushed the half-open door of the studio and that's how I found him, in a faint, his leaden head lying heavy on his arms over papers in disarray on the kitchen table where he does his drawings, in the cave beneath his loft bed, while a husky insistent voice sang *Devórame otra vez, devórame otra vez,* a voice that seemed to come from the large curly-haired head of the black Cyclops or Cyclopess on which his own hairless head was resting. For once it was not the resounding sound of Mussorgsky or Alban Berg played over and over again when he works on insomniac nights. The entire table was covered with sketches of monstrous heads. Beneath the large glass ashtray overflowing with cigarette butts, the head of a bald bearded man with eyes dilated in fear or surprise, and twisted fangs, almost like those of a wild boar, who vaguely resembles Mons. He reappeared in other pictures, almost always in discreet corners as a voyeur or an observer. I didn't know then that this was the portrait, repeated a hundred times, of his first client and to some extent his patron, who would allow him to live for an entire year in New York thanks to his only commission for a portrait *alla prima* in a single sitting. Which for Mons almost amounted to a possession, and an obsession, because he was convinced the portrait had changed his career as a painter. Sir Boar, the name Mons called him in a gamut of languages, was also portrayed on other papers scattered across the floor. The man with the twisted fang . . . It's true he resembled Mons. I also recognized the bearded head of the ogre in Tom Thumb, the living image of Mons's adoptive father, Marcel Mons, Don Marcelo to his Spanish friends, who appeared in the earliest extant sketch by Mons, drawn when he was about nine years old. Tom Thumb–Victor, at that tender age, in bed between his sleeping stepsister and stepbrother, two or three years older than he, barely pokes his head out from beneath the covers and looks with wild, terrified eyes at the ogre Mons who is about to cut their throats with a huge knife. I suppose the adoptive father never did see this drawing by his prodigy son. On one of our walks through the Grunewald Mons spoke of his adoptive father, with whom he always had problems. A few hours later I made this biostenographical note: Marcel Mons, Belgian businessman established in Madrid years before the Civil War. Patient and friend of Victor's grandfather, Dr. Verdugo—Dr. Executioner in Spanish. What's in a name? Victor Mons, in those days Victor Verdugo, was nine years old when his mother married (in 1945?) the recently widowed Mons. According to Victor, she agreed to marry the much older widower in order to please her father. A veritable Verdugo? Mons hardly knew his mother, Carmen Verdugo, when she married. Tyrannized by his stepbrother, Marcelito, and always defended by Ara, his stepsister, Mons's mother—a dark-haired beauty by Romero de Torres, he called her, whom the name Carmen suited perfectly—married three more times. She collects widowers, said Mons. She just buried the last one near Baden-Baden.

Victor . . .

I thought you were the birdman about to hit me with his stick, said Mons, while I was still shaking him by the shoulder. As usual—and he laughed—you're late. Or too early? We went to eat supper nearby, in Kreuzberg, at the Zur Kleinen Markthalle. In all the smoke and noise we found Klaus with his boisterous crowd. From time to time Mons likes to rub elbows with young artists because they haven't had time yet to develop tics, he says in his French accent, and because they remind him, I suspect, of his own irreverent youth in London when he and other uprooted artists formed part of the shocking shock troops "Artychoke." I don't remember if it was there, or maybe on the banks of the canal in Übersee, that they told us about the party other young artists were having on Friday in the Treptow Kultur-haus. Or maybe it was in one of the bars in Berlin Mitte, or Miteux, according to Mons, the calamitous Berlin we wandered in a steadily shrinking group, perhaps in Friseur, the barbershop turned into a bar, where Mons sat under a hair dryer holding a goblet in his hand and looked like a lunatic pope; or maybe on the long trip back through the taverns on Oranienstrasse. Maybe in Cazzo, where we ran into the sculptor Frieda, alias "Kahlo," who is also very young and has bushy eyebrows like a swallow's wings, whom Mons especially likes because she is lame and carries herself well. Or maybe the one who told us about the party in Treptow on Friday was Pi, the pie-eyed Catalan kid who paints only numbers—the price is the message, Mons concludes—and signs only with the letter P, whom we discovered leaning on the bar of the second camouflaged tavern in Bierhimmel, the seventh heaven of beer, across from the blond head of the barmaid who reminded Mons of the dwarf in *Las Meninas*. Bárbola at another bar . . .

Only Klaus and I remained with Mons to bid farewell to or bury the night in that crypt on Oranienstrasse, by the light of a candle in which the doll's face of the barmaid also seemed to be made of wax and the silhouettes of the Nosferatu in mourning and the acromegalic automaton in the greatcoat of a Russian soldier were flickering. The last noctambulists or somnambulists. In sinister symmetry the skulls of Nosferatu and Mons gleamed like *vanitas* as they sat, elbow to elbow, on high stools at a corner of the bar. Mons turned abruptly when he felt an intense cold on his back. The giant, still reeling with an empty glass in his hand, had ruined his jacket with vodka. We barely avoided coming to blows, but Mons already had his hands around the giant's throat. And the cadaverous mourner, who also seemed to be drunk, attempted to excuse him, explaining that he had asked Boris, who still didn't understand German very well, to offer a drink to the bald man beside him. I wasn't going to wait for him to spill another drink, and I drank mine down, the one for the road, and only Mons and Klaus were left to accept new drinks and explanations from Nosferatu—in reality his name is Hellmann, Mons seems to remember— who was an artist too, a maker of monsters and grimmlins [*sic*] that were beginning to gain acceptance in the film and entertainment industries. Delighted to show them a few, in perfect working order, and some special installations, not far at all, in Prenzlauer Berg. There is no real divergence of opinion regarding what Mons and Klaus first saw in that almost completely darkened house. But Klaus saw much less because in no time, perhaps as the result of another Bloody Mary, he was out like a light, submerged in a soft eggshell from which his blond head peered out like a pale yolk in the half-light of strange spiders that hung like lamps and moved up and down luminous threads in the rocokitsch room crowded with strange furniture and repulsive objects like the beetle or cockroach telephone that dragged itself painfully across the rug. Poor Gregor Samsa! And while he was still nodding it seemed to him that a wig or hairy round black spider smiled at him with the smile of the Cheshire cat. And maybe Mons saw what he saw in dreams?

Klaus remembers perfectly the dark courtyard, the fierce wolfhound with steaming jaws, the snow heaped in little piles, the two large tree trunks lying on the ground that made him think—there's a reason his name is Holzmann and he sculpts in wood—they would be good for his primitive Nordic couple *Askr and Embla*. He also might have thought of the painting by Mons *It Isn't Good for the Monster to Be Alone*, which depicts a Frankensteinized Adam and Eve, naked and holding hands, who looked as if they had been carved with an ax like the rough sculptures of Klaus himself. Mons had heard the complaint of Dr. Frankenstein's creature: "I am alone, terribly alone." Like the true artist, I told him, who is unique. Like each of us, Mons elaborated that night in his studio when we reviewed the text I had written for the catalogue of his next show, and again he brought to light the doubts he never kept in the dark. Did he mean: We are all unique, ergo we are all monsters? If he thought

about it, Klaus would realize that the Golem or Goliath in
the greenish greatcoat also had bangs, no doubt to accen-
tuate the resemblance. He also recalled, as did Mons, that
when he entered the first room, narrow and almost completely dark, on the first floor, he was suddenly terrified and
almost scorched by an iron dragon with rusted scales that
spun around belching flames like a blowtorch. Nidhogg,
Hellmann told them. It's plausible that Klaus, so well versed
in Nordic mythology, then explained to Mons that this was
the dragon that sucks the blood of the damned in the world
of darkness, or Niflheim. He did not, however, recall the
motorcyclist dressed in tight black leather and a helmet with
painted serpents who came in, shaking off the snow, went
behind a screen to change, and emerged transformed into
the statuesque albino girl in a white tunic, white as a statue,
who led Mons by the hand into the depths of the house. And
he also did not recall a kind of resting place dimly lit by can-
dles in wall sconces, with mattresses on the floor where
apparently sleeping men and women of differing ages lay in
a promiscuous jumble. They are traveling, Mons says Hellmann said. Among those sorrowful shamans and grieving
household gods he recognized the tiny old woman with the
black cap and sharp-featured parchmentlike face, the very
same cadaverously pale lady he and I had seen a few nights
earlier at an ashen assemblage in a trendy new bistro near
Savignyplatz. We had been struck by her pallor even before
she lay stiff and rigid on the floor while her companion, a
dark, slender young woman with very short hair, who may
have resembled her, kneeled at her side and tried to revive
her. An impassive waitress told us they would take care of
her shortly. She lay there unmoving on black and white

squares while the other diners, embarrassed only at first, went on and on and—yes—we went on chewing. Life is for the living. . . . We did, in fact, believe she was dead. The dark girl, who was very young, did not leave her side. Until the ambulance arrived, preceded by some ugly old birds of evil omen, funereal, very pale, all of them, men and women, dressed in black, who did not pass beyond the restaurant door but seemed to be lying in wait, scratching at the window behind me with a scraping of their nails that still makes my blood run cold. Devils, that's what Mons called them, and I remember we ended up discussing whether the Devil or God was the greater monster. Since the Devil cannot be the Creator, a divine attribute, God permits him to possess artists, those minuscule parodies of the Creator. If only I were God . . . , the Devil says to himself, for he would like to be the greater monster. Arguments of Mons, theoheretical, when viewing an all-too-present body lying in state. Mons insists she is the very same pale lady who I said resembled— Mons has a very good memory—a certain Baroness Blitzen, a thundering bolt from the blue; but for him she brought to mind—especially because of her extremely white skin and delicate build, for he never did see her face—an old acquaintance who, however, was or seemed to be young. And after the meal, encouraged by generous amounts of cognac, he expounded, expanded on, I would say, the extraordinary chronicle of his first portrait on human skin.

And Klaus had not visited the installation or great square bunker whose walls were television screens, with a robot totem of television sets piled one on top of the other in the center (and eyes—a fly's eyes—that were multilensed) and duplicated in each one of those mirrors. Or the projection room—perhaps in a basement, because Mons believes he descended stairs in the dark still holding the icy hand of the white lady—where King Kong examined, in the palm of his huge black hand, the Lilliputian blond who looked like Eva Braun made up to look like Greta Garbo and, hands clasped, pleaded with the Chaplinesque shadow on the screen that leaped and loomed, larger and larger, hands clapping. *Heil!* He had seen it seventeen times! Mons says Hellmann said.

And in that dark room Mons also saw the white phosphorescence of a palpitating translucent veil that moved through the abysmal blackness by contracting and dilating like a diaphanous heart with its systole and diastole in the rhythmic wake of the dance of the veil of the Medusa who enveloped him, undulating like the white lady writhing on the deep black divan, gently caressing his belly with her albino hair and breathing him into the icy depths where he thought he could see two staring eyes and sighing as she covered him with her wide transparent white tunic that became the silken throw of Helen Gulick, who covered him, laughing, after taking him by surprise in bed centuries ago in London, Mons recalled, and Helen really became his Medusa Made in the USA, as he called her, a hyperrealistic sculptor who was a classmate of John de Andrea, when Mons found her one night sleeping on the floor of her studio-shed on the docks, among all those statues of salt or fiberglass, or perhaps Pompeians petrified where they stood by sudden lava or by her glance of a sculpting Medusa, with whom he shared more than one model (in *Grâce à trois* the graceful naked blond, arm in arm with the Rubenesque Helen and Mons, contemplates the painting and the sculpture at the rear of the studio that depict her as a Grace spreading her arms over the nonexistent shoulders of the two missing Graces) and who eventually petrified herself in the mirror of the night—*The Sleeper* dressed only in the reflections of neon lights flashing through a window—long before she went to her eternal rest in New York after a cocktail of veronalcohol, a blond barbituric Barbie doll who wrapped herself again in her white winding sheet and dissolved into profound blackness, dancing with her transparent veils in the phosphorescence of a blinking television screen that intermittently illuminated the whitened room where the dryad swayed alone with raised arms and hands that had roots for nails, her hair like a dark veil over her face, her body slight and copper-colored, her breasts like apples, who seemed to be the fine arts student Anne Kiefer, he was certain, and who disappeared in a whirlwind of dust down a gloomy hall that led to a room with an iron bed and a bidet, separated by a heavy curtain from a cubicle reddened by a brazier where the naked vampire Eva loosens her fiery red hair over the scruffy adolescent Adam who kneels and sobs in her arms. Hidden among the folds of the heavy red curtain he believed he recognized that bald voyeur with the goatee who licks his lips and shows his tusks. . . . And Klaus did not get as far as the buffet, a long table covered with plates of cold meats and bottles presided over by an enormous pannikin of bread or *pain-surprise* that should have been filled with sandwiches and from which there emerged, when the cover was lifted, *nain-surprise!* a dwarf in a cloak with a dagger at his waist. But Mons would begin to wonder if he hadn't really seen that pannikin manikin or Peter Pan the following day at the buffo buffet at the party in Treptow. And Klaus wasn't sure if he had seen silhouettes and shadows in the long hall of the house in Prenzlauer Berg, going into and out of other rooms, some of them illuminated. Or the dark hassock that turned out to be a large snake that coiled and uncoiled, said Mons, under the low glass table on which fresh drinks were served to them. Klaus recalls that his head was spinning and without too much dissimulation he poured the new Bloody Mary into a large ashtray on a tripod. It isn't right to sprinkle blood on ashes, was Hellmann's macabre joke. That's what Mons said Hellmann said, but Klaus doesn't recall that either. Or the two shadow figures quivering as they coupled behind a screen, or what Mons says Hellmann said after a loud guffaw: Peter Schlemiel and the Woman Without a Shadow are making the beast with two backs. Neither Beast nor Angel. Or the other goods, chattels, entities, and enigmas Mons saw or says he saw that night in the house in Prenzlauer Berg and would remember dimly at dawn, back in his dilapidated studio—and calvary—in Kreuzberg, before confronting his own monsters:

The tortoise with the head and chest of a woman, a pearl necklace over her swelling breasts, saying *pian piano* to the scorpion with the legs and feet of a man who stung her as he plucked her *viola d'amore*.

The female centaur who grasped her breasts with both hands and shook her hair, tied back in a charming ponytail, as she was penetrated by a goat-bearded faun riding astride her rump to service her and exclaiming, joyful and perspiring, when he finished: We'll make a fauntaur! And this was celebrated with a raised champagne glass by the bearded minotaur reclining on pillows next to a naked blond bacchante who—cautious or envious—limited herself to pointing an index finger at her right eye: *Mon œil!*

The woman with double pupils ablaze with rage that shot out laser beams as she flicked a vibrating forked tongue between tattooed lips, writhing all the while like a snake.

The terrible African woman or goddess dripping blood and whirling around, impaled on a spear, and changing her terrifying face or mask with each turn.

The bestial cannibal giant Grendel, encrusted with mud, advancing on all fours to his encounter with the coal-black cannibal Caliban, who roared as he looked at himself in a puddle and raised his head, pacified, when he heard the seraphic aria of the Phantom of the Opera offering his golden mask, brilliant with tears, for him to use as a mirror.

And he would see again on the wall of his studio the grotesque silhouette of the masked figure with a reindeer's antlers, the eyes and beak of an owl, a bearded man's large head, the forefeet of a lion, and a horse's hooves and tail, a figure that leaped, trembled, roared, scratched, kicked, and was the shadow of a frantic Mons as he gave himself over to the destruction of his monsters.

I tried to imagine him: raging in fury, fighting tooth and nail with his Gorgons, rip rend rupture raze, papers fabrics easels struck and stamped on, more kicks to the bearded manticore that looks like me, despite its lion's body, even butting with his hard clean-shaven bare head the mottled Minotaur monstrous in black, clearing away with his feet the triturated tritons, satyrs in shreds, splintered Cyclops, fauns and centaurs in a hundred pieces, another chimera cut down, pow, another slash and a decapitated Janus doesn't even complain. . . . Agghhh. And to think I will never again see my three faces of a bestial Janus that resembled a wolf man, a royal lion, and a bulldog, or perhaps a cretin, a fanatic, and a brute, and reminded me of Titian's *Signum Triciput,* which I admired so often in the National Gallery in London, though Mons insisted he had been inspired by Grünewald's *Trias Romana,* which is here in Berlin in the Küpferstichkabinett, and besides, they weren't faces of my face, damn it! There's no longer any point to that discussion. After committing his predawn *crime passionnel* or genocide— if we can call it that—against his monsters, Mons probably could not bear to sleep in his lion's den, so suddenly empty, or perhaps he preferred an immediate change of scene, as he always did when he was about to begin a new phase, and that same morning he went to the Hotel Askanischer Hof, where he had stayed during his first weeks in Berlin. He returned to the spacious room with the double sliding doors and large window like a triptych overlooking the Ku'damm, number 12 on the second floor, a comfortable, old-fashioned room with tapestries and carpets that reminded me of the studio of a successful academic painter at the end of the last century. It could have been the studio of John Singer Sargent in Paris—I told him this time—if it weren't for the television. And Mons, sprawled calmly in a spectacular black leather swivel armchair with his feet on a footrest, observed that the television set occupied the place of the easel. But this furniture, and I, are from the 1930s, he added, and he seemed very serene when he stated that there had been no crime of passion when he destroyed his *Monstruary.* Rather, he said, it had been a mercy killing. A terrible new beauty is reborn, he announced, and he picked up the tablet that was on the television and smiled enigmatically as he handed me the pencil sketch he had completed shortly before my arrival: a vibration of black and white bands, almost like op art, that

formed, when you looked closely, a sinuous feminine silhouette undulating in a transparent box, perhaps an aquarium. It
pleased him to see me so intrigued by his "Dame X." His
Dame de la Ku'damm. Drawn from life, he said. And he
showed her to me through the window: a strange, if not terrible, beauty, the brunette with very short hair as black as her
eyes, heavily outlined with kohl, her fine-featured, vaguely
Egyptian profile, somewhere between Nefertiti and Audrey
Hepburn, though Mons didn't see it, rather hieratic as she
sat half turned, her sturdy cylindrical slenderness in a tight
tubular minidress with brilliant horizontal black and white
bands, like her stockings, and her bangs with albinic streaks,
and a small handbag and leather jacket at her feet, on the
straw-covered floor of the glass box atop a cement cube in
the middle of the wide sidewalk of the Ku'damm, almost at
the door of the hotel, in a line with other glass boxes dis-
playing a wide variety of deluxe articles. Doesn't she seem
live? And in fact, I didn't miss the fact that at the top of the
four glass walls of the case large black letters spelled VIVA—
live, in Spanish—two minutes from there, according to three
little arrows $\rightarrow$ $\rightarrow$ $\rightarrow$, *2 Min. von hier,* at Schlüterstrasse 36.
The cement bases of these Ku'damm boxes were covered
with graffiti, and on the one that held the lady mannequin,
and copied faithfully by Mons, HIKE was scrawled in white
spray paint, I suppose in English, I don't know whether to
indicate walking or some increase in prices, and I thought it
an exaggerated piece of camouflage to have the demoiselle
sit on straw considering the in-no-way rustic prices her
striped clothes would bring in the shop called Viva. Long live
the line! I was about to exclaim. The lively bands in Mons's

drawing made me think of a Matisse odalisque in harem trousers, but a peristaltic one, a zealous zebra undulating in a sinuous dance simultaneously attractive and repulsive. You think so? And he arched his heavy eyebrows into an M. I'll have to draw her again. *Eva Prima Pandora,* in her box, was the title I suggested. But *primum vivere,* the artist does not live by bread or Pandora's boxes alone, and he suggested I go with him to eat with Double Uwe. He surely thought I would be his lightning rod. . . . At first Double Uwe believed Mons was joking when, without losing his smile or his appetite, he told him all about it in the Paris Bar. Until Double Uwe choked, about to burst his seams. Dribbling bearnaise sauce or slaver down his chin. Can you believe it, Emil? But Double Uwe was in no mood to listen to anybody and spoke about Mons as if he weren't there in front of him. He has a fit, and wham! he tosses months and months of work overboard! Almost overboard—into a container beside the Landwehr Kanal. So many days and nights! measurable only in the measureless fury of frenetic, obsessive work. On the back wall, hanging almost over the head of Double Uwe, a vestige—a small sanguinolent sketch—of the works and nights of Mons: the ravenous Goyaesque ogre with raving eyes gnawing his own feet, holding on to his legs with both hands, bent almost in two. Cronos coiled. Mons endured the rantings of Double Uwe without blinking an eye. And his show? For which I had started to write the catalogue . . . But Double Uwe began to yield when Mons casually mentioned a new project, maybe, we'll see, *Dame de la Ku'damm,* always the same, always different, different angles, kaleidoscopic, *la bella donna è mobile!* I observed enthusiastically. And then

I described for him the first *dame* I had seen at the hotel. Double Uwe wanted to see her too, immediately, but Mons declared that he preferred to show him several, in a few days. If there are going to be several . . . , he murmured doubtfully. As we were saying good-bye at the door of the restaurant, Mons told me I should stop by Filmbühne that night. He would be there with Klaus and his crew from the Steinplatz School of Fine Arts. Double Uwe and I watched him walk away, with his nervous strides and his head like a punching bag above his black overcoat, along Kantstrasse, until he turned right onto Savignyplatz. No doubt he was returning to the hotel to study his encased *dame* from his observatory. *Belle dame* . . . She showed him no mercy. And almost turned him to stone when he saw her again that night on his way to his appointment in Steinplatz: flesh and blood, plying her trade on the corner of Ku'damm and Knesebeckstrasse. In the same white-and-black-striped dress and jacket. Her dazzling white-and-black ass shapely in stretch fabric as she bent over to chat with the driver of a black BMW. I was very close to her, said Mons, when she walked quickly around the car and got in next to the driver. A deal as fast as the car. A deluxe whore who buys or is given fashions from Viva. Or a cheap whore with expensive clothes. This one was more attractive, he said, and more solid than the original mannequin. When Mons told us, in Filmbühne, that he had just seen a whore on the Ku'damm in the same flashy dress worn by Pandora in her box, he was truly excited. I have to paint her, he said, from life. Live to the painted canvas . . . He thought he had freed himself from his imaginary monsters, and we didn't suspect they'd be up to their old tricks that very night. And in spite of the accident—or was it a surprise attack?—Double Uwe is hopeful that Mons will reconstruct his monsters. Or a single monster in its various metamorphoses? After the rest cure. Double Uwe is his Berlin dealer but demonstrates that he's even prepared to become his nurse. Or watchdog: Uwe Wach as *Wachhund*. Following the emergency treatment and tests in a Charlottenburg hospital, he arranged to move Mons to this private sanitarium on the edge of the Wannsee, in Am Grossen Wannsee, which looks more like a villa on the Riviera. Dr. Koppel will make you as good as new, he assured him optimistically.

Very soon, very soon . . . , we thought he was saying in French shortly after the nurse who had frightened him left, and it really was too soon for us to understand that he was repeating, almost muzzled by his bandages: Treptow . . . With growing impatience he tried to explain that he had seen the redheaded girl again—or was she Petra?—from the terrace of the Kulturhaus in Treptow and then in the snow-covered park in Treptow, with the bronze Russian soldier. Bronze? Mons traveled back in time to the party at Treptow, but now he stayed calm despite what he was reliving. Or seeing. On—one might say—a dark television screen sprinkled with snow. He could see it all again in intermittent flashes, even with his eyes closed:

The dark winged silhouette lengthening across the sky toward the icy ring around the moon, its roar growing louder.

The brilliant light (of a storm? a fire?) on the horizon, toward the River Spree and beyond the fine black lace of treetops haloed in gold and ocher.

Black silhouettes of horsemen galloping among the black

stripes of tree trunks and, in a sudden flash, the gleam of a helmet with the head of Medusa, serpents bristling.

A great red dragon with Fra-angelic wings, human arms, and a coiled serpent's tail, vomiting red-plumed tongues of blood and flame as it cut across the night.

The trampling angel with the body of curling clouds who plunges ahead on petrified pillar legs that shoot fire like muskets and make the earth tremble to the rhythm of a pile driver.

Ill-assorted multitudes of human figures with the heads of animals, vertebrate and invertebrate, and all kinds of beasts and insects with the heads of men and women and mutants, semihuman masses that swarm like ant colonies, surge like cresting waves, spill like avalanches into chasms of darkness.

Clusters of whitish and yellowish homunculi rushing headlong into a hopper of live coals.

Demons with bodies covered in excretions and excrescences, mineral and vegetable, and cockscombs of excrement and coral and lichens, jumbled together in uproarious confusion.

The smiling creature with the feline head topped with a tiara, who sits on a throne and has large breasts and for genitalia a bearded, open-mouthed little head between spraddled he-goat's legs that end in a rooster's claws and spurs. (As he leafed through a bulky volume of fantastical tales and images in a bookstore on London's Cecil Court in the early 1970s, Mons immediately recognized, he said, the strange demon who had made such a strong impression on him almost thirty years earlier, in a black book from his grandfather's library, which he closed hurriedly and would never open again, he said, because it disappeared as if by magic. It was probably a borrowed book, he deduced, or his grandfather had put it out of the reach of his innocent hands. In any case, the print was truly imprinted in his brain.)

The mountain with the head of a mature bald man, black brows peaked in an M, which was a caricature of himself. Or perhaps of Michel de Montaigne?

Mountain of Mons? Teufelsberg, the Devil's mountain, like the peaked shadow projected by a high, pensive gargoyle.

The living portrait of Mons? Bald head and sparse beard, sallow skin and staring bloodshot eyes almost bulging out of their sockets, the tusks of a wild boar visible in the light of a fire, the portrait pressed against her naked belly by a skinny she-devil who shook her legs—sheathed in black stockings— as she jumped or danced over the flames.

A gigantic head with tiny legs, the head of Immanuel Kant.

A group of dwarves in which he recognized Toulouse-Lautrec and Georg Christoph Lichtenberg. *Mehr Lichtenberg!* shouted a homunculus before disappearing into the darkness.

A sickly-looking hunchback in a Spanish cape brandishing his sword and shouting Change is for the better, and in a swirl of his cape he was transformed into a crippled musketeer dwarf with long hair and a goatee who announced in French: I am Achilles the painter of nimble feet, I am almost emperor, before he whirled again and turned back into the hunchback in the Spanish cape who resembled, Mons thought, the Spanish-Mexican playwright Ruiz de

Alarcón. The suspect truth is that as a child Mons had lived on a street in Madrid with that name, behind the Plaza de Cibeles. *Je suis Achille!* the musketeer insisted. *Le menteur . . .*

A huge-headed dwarf with a flattened nose flush with his eyebrows, squatting like an Aztec idol, looking at himself in a double mirror opened like a book on the ground. An encephalic Narcissus . . . (As a child Mons would sneak looks at the monsters in some of his grandfather's medical books. And in others, naked women, witches, demons.)

A heavy-jowled toad, its pustular skin pitted by purulent craters, that resembled Martin Luther.

A giant starling straddled by a naked Lilliputian.

A grasshopper wearing an African mask.

A tightrope walker with the head of a goldfinch.

A carp with the head of a duck.

A beetle with the gaunt, dissipated face of a young man.

Fish with human arms, men and women with fishtails, and in the uncertain aquarium light one could not tell if they were in a glass box or on the other side.

Inside the box a strangely equine dragon's head with a staring amber eye and gaping fiery mouth.

Behind the black cloud—it made his hair stand on end— a gigantic mane of pythons. Branching out nervously in the foam as it raises and coils enormous tentacles around its wet gray head, two fat drops of black ink still trembling in its eyes, it rises from the depths of childhood—from a market and that awful book on the wonders of the sea—to rekindle once again the terror of an embrace that ended in a crackling of bones that the scratch of pen on paper would reproduce with the distant crackling of Kraken.

An octopus pulled itself along the tiled floor to the

cowering naked woman with the dark topknot and pubis, trapped against the wall, to surround her with its tentacles and bend her back and lay her down adorned with its necklaces of suckers, and, finally, panting, bury its large viscous head in her groin. And Mons still recalled the attraction and repulsion the grayish mass produced in him, that immense elastic glob of phlegm distending on a table in the market, extending and twisting its tentacles, a viscous knot that suddenly took on a drab brownish coloring.

The immense liquid eye of the black Cyclopess drawing him into its depths.

Those visions occurred one after the other as he pondered *Monstruary* on his walks through the Grunewald wood—which he pronounced as if it were French: Grünewald—but in reality (reality?) he was in the park at Treptow lying in the snow at the end of a far too immoderate night.

The roar or clamor moved away with the dragon that hid behind a cloud and reemerged as an airplane.

At first he thought, Mons recounted, that he was still dreaming at the kitchen table in his studio and that I hadn't come in yet to wake him.

He was numb with cold, not feeling his own body, said Mons, and though he lay faceup he could see it detached like a dark hide or an elongated, motionless shadow on the snow.

That's how we finally found him, Klaus and I, lying in front of the catafalque at the Soviet memorial in Treptow Park, after tracking him for quite some time—we saw him rush out of the party at the Kulturhaus as if the Devil were at his heels—and following him along Puschkinallee and losing sight of him and seeing him again in the distance in Treptow Park. Just as well that in his black overcoat he stood out like an inkblot on the blanket of snow. That night we had all had too much to drink, again, and with a good deal of slipping and stumbling Klaus and I managed to get Mons to Klaus's new jalopy—his antediluvian Trabant—and take him back to the hotel. Mons said he had gone out on the terrace of the Kulturhaus to clear his head and was looking at the spectral whiteness of the snow in the moonlight when he thought he saw Petra-Petrushka, or her living redheaded likeness down below, leaving the dance, laughing, hanging on the arm of the giant in the Russian greatcoat or his double. Without saying good-bye to us, he found his coat in the cloakroom and—luckily Klaus saw him at this point—ran out into the black-and-white night to follow them, at first along Hoffmannstrasse, but he lost sight of them and went back toward Puschkinallee and spotted them in the distance—the flame of her hair a red ignis fatuus guiding him through the night to Treptow Park—and followed their footsteps in the snow along the great esplanade as white as a winding sheet under which several thousand Soviet soldiers stand at ease, their distant silhouettes still there in the narrow pass between reddish blocks of marble that are supposed to represent two lowered flags and, according to Mons, look more like two gigantic sphinxes face-to-face, and then it seemed to him that the giant in the greatcoat was by himself as he climbed the stairs leading to the top of the catafalque and went into the vault or mausoleum above which looms the gigantic Russian soldier who holds a child in his left arm and with his right points a sword at the swastika lying broken at his feet. Mons said he remembered then that Petra told him the only memory she had of her father was of a giant in uniform—the Russian unknown soldier—who lifted her high, very high, in his arms. Did her father take her to Treptow Park when she was little? The girl with the red hair and black jacket—Mons recalled—stood alone looking at the giant soldier or at the vault her companion had entered. And Mons would have sworn the bronze soldier worshiping in front of the marble flag, the one on the right, moved. He looked again at the bronze soldier—a snow soldier by then—whose left knee is on the ground as he holds an upright machine gun in his right hand and a helmet in his left. A good piece of work in the Stalinist style. And Petra petrified there in front of the catafalque (or was it someone else?). And suddenly a tremendous clamor in the sky and—vertigo? While the Trabant trembled toward the Ku'damm, shaken by our laughter, Klaus and I argued whether the soldier hit Mons on the head with his helmet or the butt of his machine gun, and Mons settled the matter sensibly by saying that what really hit him was the vodka. And decided to get out on Georg-Grosz-Platz—I always get out here, he insisted—and walk the few meters to the Hotel Askanischer Hof for a breath of polar air. We left him—and we shouldn't have—walking on leaden feet along the icy sidewalk to the hotel. A few meters from the hotel, on the corner of Wielandstrasse and the Ku'damm, he again ran into the peripatetic *dame* in the brilliant white-and-black dress, walking somewhat unsteadily and brushing against the glass cases. Mons recalls the smell of alcohol and her listless laugh Ah! ah! ah! when he bumped into her. The laugh was also recalled by the night clerk at the Hotel Askanischer Hof who heard it, along with panting and the sound of footsteps on the stairs, even before he saw—with disapproving eyes—Herr Mons enter the lobby carrying the lady in his arms while she muffled her laugh Ah! ah! ah! against Mons's neck, both of them wrapped in his long black muffler. It was obvious to the receptionist that they were high. Mons recalls that as soon as they entered the room he fell with her onto the bed, and what with rushing and struggling to get undressed they ended up rolling onto the floor and laughing all over again. Her dress, so tight, was slippery like her, or so it seemed to him, elastic and brilliant, with black and white bands, like her stockings with their scales brilliant in the gray light of dawn coming in through the window; she writhed sinuously (or was she resisting?), but at last he managed to pull off one stocking, like a second skin, and then the other, a snakeskin, one might say, two snakeskins on the rug, twisting and recovering their flexible, agile, compact form, Ah! ah! ah! a yearning breath ending in a whistle, and they rose toward Mons, who saw the solid ringed body of the great white-and-black snake that raised its aggressive head with a vibrant swaying and flicked its tongue, transfixing him with eyes of glass. It glided and ascended with its automaton's swaying. And Mons said his terror was unbearable, he saw himself as a solitary Laocoön, he said, attacked and entrapped by enraged snakes that would coil around his neck and arms while he was paralyzed with terror and the yearning breath came closer with that muted slithering hiss of glass, its head the head of an arrow ready to fly, ready to sink its fangs into his neck, and in a leap he reached the window and without a moment's hesitation threw himself head-first onto the Ku'damm. Fortunately yours is hard, said Double Uwe. You bet. No one can get it into Mons's head that he had to be the one who broke the glass case on the Ku'damm and carried the mannequin into the hotel. The corpus delicti—or delirii—was irrefutable proof: the mannequin lay half-undressed on the floor of Room 12. The tubular dress was pulled up to her chest, but the curious thing is that her stockings were nowhere to be found. Mons must have thrown them out the window, though he doesn't recall doing it. Double Uwe promptly paid for everything at the boutique on Schlüterstrasse, including the life-size doll in her skimpy white-and-black dress—which vaguely resembles the rings of a krait cobra—because Mons has asked that she be taken to his studio so he can paint her again—when he recovers and they remove the bandages—as he has just said—of the Mummy or the Invisible Man.

# Mons Veneris

A DAME of the Ku'damm, or rather a clothed *maja* still wearing her white-and-black skirt and hunting jacket but no stockings: that was the mannequin we left, limp and lifeless, on the one-armed divan or ottomanqué in Mons's studio.

On the morning he was discharged we accompanied him from the hospital to his studio, above all to see how he would react. The gentleman with hand (bandaged) on chest (bandaged). Fortunately, he's left-handed. We're both pretty sinister, I recall him telling me long ago (almost a quarter of a century) in a London pub, The Man in the Moon, when he saw me making notes; but he quickly added: though you don't look it. In any case, he'd be capable of painting with his feet. Or his mouth, holding the pen between his teeth, as I saw him do one night in the Café Strada when he drew the likeness of the painter Adalbert Stock who, from the other side of the table, watched in amazement and amusement as, feature by feature, his large bearded minotaur's head appeared on the tablecloth. Mons did not seem too happy to be back in his studio, his scowl in a typical ill-humored M. It's true that his entire body still pained him. And possibly the destruction of his monsters. Didn't he recognize her? Ruby lips and ivory teeth . . . For atmosphere we had even put on the cassette of "Beautiful Doll," the prosthesis song, Mons

3 5

called it, the one his mother had listened to, turned very low on migraine afternoons, among so many dimly lit tangos, he said, reclining on a sofa in the living room of her Madrid apartment with a cologne-soaked handkerchief on her forehead, while he drew battles, lying on the floor in the ray of sun that filtered through the closed shutters of the balcony. But he could also draw in the dark and with his eyes closed, a technique he still uses in the blind spontaneity of the sketches he calls interiors. When his mother had a headache, Mons recounted, she always had him draw. Drawing tames wild beasts . . . We probably owe Mons's artistic calling to Doña Carmen's migraines.

His mistrustful air. Had we taken him by surprise? Didn't he recall asking us for the doll of his skull-shattering misfortune? He looked at her as if he didn't recognize her, there on the red ottoman where so many models have posed for him, and told us to take her away. To Klaus Holzmann's tiny room just around the corner. And one night on a pub crawl—without Mons—we carried her from Bar to Bar Centrale, hitting every one from Kreuzberg to Savignyplatz. There's a photograph of Klaus sitting with the mannequin at a table in the Rosalinde. They both seem to be looking with interest at the passersby on Knesebeckstrasse. I tried in vain to persuade Mons to paint a self-portrait with doll, a replica of his portrait of the painter Oskar Kokoschka. He had met Kokoschka in London in the early sixties, and a small quid pro quo may have facilitated their first encounter in an office at the Tate Gallery. Kokoschka thought his young admirer was named Moos and asked if he had family in Stuttgart. Moos, moss or—maybe—mazuma long and green, simply by changing a letter or two . . . Mons knew all about the doll, but until then he hadn't heard of a marionette maker in Stuttgart called Moos. He was so intrigued by the singular story of the "silent woman," the life-sized doll the resentful painter had ordered in 1918 from Miss Hermine Moos, which would become, following their breakup, the soulless body—*el cuerpo sin alma*—of Alma Mahler, her pluperfect double, *plus vrai que nature,* that Mons included her as a menacing lover, almost a praying mantis, sprawled or lying disjointed on a sofa next to Kokoschka, who rigidly sits and looks at her in profile, his mouth partially open. The doll's dark hair seems stained with trickles of blood. Alma's poor double, after serving as Kokoschka's model, came to a bad end. She enlivened a wild party Kokoschka gave in his house in Dresden, and at dawn they threw her tattered remains into the garden. Kokoschka even broke a bottle of red wine over her head. Poor Almannequin! Mons's portrait suggested that perhaps the painter had regretted his rage and rescued his fatal doll when the festivities were over. This interpretation did not please Mons. Besides, he was not prepared to follow in the footsteps of his master Kokoschka. He said that the mannequin, removed from her nocturnal case, lost her charm. The *maja* lost her magic. And he preferred to paint the little *dame* of the Ku'damm from memory. Speaking of magic and *majas,* of mad, foolish things, on another night when we were walking on the Ku'damm near the glass case in front of the Hotel Askanischer Hof (they had changed the mannequin and the costume), Klaus, forever meandering in mythologies, mentioned that the word HIKE spray-painted in white on the cement base (it was still there) probably wasn't English but an ancient Egyptian formula signifying magical power. Damn! A Nefertitionette!

Klaus had better be careful, she was already installed in his den. I, however, noticed that beneath the window of the room Mons usually occupies at the Hotel Askanischer Hof there is a shop sign that says, in gold letters, PATRICK HELL-MANN. Hadn't Mons said that the Nosferatu in the house of monsters in Prenzlauer Berg was named Hellmann? I didn't mention it so he wouldn't say that I'm the one who goes around warping words and misconstruing idle chatter. But I believe that if Mons soon tired of the Pandora of the Ku'damm, it was not only because of the recent unhappy memories she brought back to him, but because of other memories that are much older. And much more painful. Not only Petra, his transvestite Petrushka from Tamara Karsavina, his Russian or half-Russian doll, his Wigged-out Wig, who disappeared when he still needed her in Berlin to replace his antonomastic doll and Eva the First, Eva Lalka, his Polish girl from London, lost twenty years before. I would sometimes see them in the afternoon in Daquise, the Polish café and restaurant in South Kensington. She was tall and slender, very attractive of her type, somewhere between a transvestite and an epicene ephebe though her small ass and tits were prominent, sitting beside the stocky bald man with the polished skull and Mephistophelian goatee. She began to be successful as a model, but the Doll had intellectual pretensions and posed in Daquise, almost always with some book on her table—in English and in French—by her compatriot Witold Gombrowicz. I recall one afternoon when she asked me if I had ever set foot in Patagonia, showed me photographs of guanacos and gauchos, and told me how she would love to photograph the places in Buenos Aires where Gombrowicz had lived in exile for almost a quarter of a century. The streets—Corrientes, Tucumán, Tacuari, Bacacay—sounded so exotic to her. And in a way she resembled one of Gombrowicz's false, awkward adolescent boys. She even looked a little like the adolescent Gombrowicz in the picture cut from a Polish magazine that she used as a bookmark in her tattered copy of *Ferdydurke*. I didn't know at the time that she aspired to go beyond the objective. Though I frequently saw her face and figure on poster advertisements in the tube and on the streets of London, no one portrayed her so turbid and perturbing as Mons, black eyes so large and deep in the misty whiteness of her fine-featured face with its burnished cheekbones.

She was model and lover, but she refused to lose her independence. She agreed to live in Mons's house, on Queensberry Place, provided she would keep the room in Camden Town that was her photography studio. Through scattered confidences of Mons, confessions over the rim of a glass of what was truly bitter, almost always in World's End, the last pub in our crawl from Fulham Road (Queen's Elm) to King's Road, I reconstructed the successive deaths and rebirths of a passion that became increasingly painful for Mons. She frequently went out at night without Mons and sometimes did not come back for several days. Surprisingly, she was willing to answer, with complete crudity or cruelty and in exact, explicit detail, the pointless paranoic police interrogations to which Mons subjected her, at times for hours. Hours of interminable agony, Mons said, and of humiliation. Though in reality—one also paints with pain—they proved productive. One night when Eva had slipped away again, Mons showed me a series of sketches in charcoal and pastels that I found extremely moving for their perfection and perversity, and for the confidence in me they once again demonstrated. I recalled then that not long after we met, when Mons had his studio in Notting Hill Gate, I saw the portrait of a woman's face as white as a death mask, with shadowed eyes and sensual lips slightly parted in an enigmatic smile, and I asked who she was. Edmonde in her bath of death an hour and a half after cutting the veins in her wrists and at the back of her knees with a Gillette razor blade. A forensic answer. So as to seem precise. As he would try to be when he made the drawing with a steady hand, leaning over his dead wife. In the sketch you don't see the tub, only a whiteness that looks like a pillow beneath her black hair. Surely he drew it as he watched over Edmonde's body in the bedroom. Mons had done several paintings of Edmonde lying naked and languid in an old tub in a bathroom with black and white tiles, enveloped in the vaporous ambience of Bonnard's *bon art*. But his most intense portrait of Edmonde, or of the mark left by her absence, is the one called *The Red Bathtub*, which seems to contain a Rothko, with all that red blood of her suicide. It happened on the farm they had near Paris, in a village in the region of Vexin called Enfer, no less, which Mons has kept because he says that when he paints there he can't cheat, he claims he works like a condemned man who has nothing left to win or lose. I remember my first, somber, wintry impression of the farm in Enfer: two large, gray, shabby buildings separated by a dirt courtyard and surrounded by a high, gated wall, at the edge of a dark forest. On the chemin d'Avernes, in the plural, to intensify the infernal atmosphere. I was convinced that Mons chose the place primarily for the name. But hell is or can be anywhere. Mons burned in it, in London, when he showed me the series of drawings inspired by Eva Lalka, his model and demon. Her diabolical beauty . . . I don't know whether to call them *The Greatest Monster* or *The Painter of his Own Dishonor,* Mons said dramatically as he spread on the table the drawings in which Eva Lalka, always the same Eva in different poses, copulated with a variety of men, always observed by the same voyeur, who portrayed them. Each scene must have reproduced one that Eva had recounted in his successive interrogations:

Eva in black stockings, sitting at the head of an unmade iron bed, grasps in her left hand the erect, imposing member of the slender naked man lying faceup at her side, both of them watched by the bald man, dimly reflected in the mirror of the armoire, who is drawing them from behind some draperies.

Eva, chalk white and on all fours, impales herself on the stalwart black who lies on the floor and clasps her buttocks, while from the half-opened door a bald man draws them, sketchbook in hand.

Eva held aloft by two identical, naked, athletic blacks: the one on the left holds her thighs and enters her while the one on the right supports her under her right arm and with his left hand is about to penetrate her ass with an ebony shaft or staff magnified by charcoal into an enormous bludgeon in the sketchbook in which the bald man, one knee on the ground and half-hidden behind some cactus plants, is drawing.

Eva bending over and almost swallowing the member of a brawny bruiser who stands and holds her head with both hands while another man, younger and slimmer, penetrates her ass with a priapic phallus attached to his scrotum, a few steps from the bald man who sits in an armchair and faithfully copies the felicitous fellatio into a sketchbook that rests on his knees.

The skinny man in the blue turban, his face and torso tan, the fly of his jeans opened to reveal a scarlet needleprick, very thin and pointed, which Eva, kneeling in black panties, holds in her left hand and places between her breasts, so white, so small, so pert, her right hand encircling his waist, while they are observed from the armchair by the bald man, barely visible except for a segment of his skull and beard. The voyeur may once again be Mons or resemble him, but perhaps he was identified with an anonymous voyeur, hidden in an easy chair, whose face Eva never really saw when she was doing yoga or *Kama-sutra* exercises with a Pakistani who worked at a gambling house in Bayswater. Eva suspected that the voyeur was the owner of the gambling house, a man of German origin, though he disappeared before she could stand up. She also told Mons that when she began to work as a model, she met a photographer from Chelsea who constantly asked to hide and photograph her making love in her studio, without her partner's knowledge. You don't think I was capable . . . , and she burst into laughter when Mons asked who did you do it with.

Eva lying on the floor, her legs in an M, offering the open crack of her cunt to the man with spiral tattoos on his skull who leans over her belly and holds in his left hand an awl that brushes against her pubis . . . The oil is unfinished, and Mons pointed out that Eva abruptly stopped the session because she thought he was trying to tattoo her. She was going to supper with some friends shortly afterward and hurried away without waiting for his explanations. That was when

Mons became particularly interested in the art of tattooing and showed Eva a book of photographs of Maori tattooed from head to toe. Those living pictograms were not to her liking. She didn't come back for almost a week, said Mons, who went looking for her, without success, in the places in Chelsea, Notting Hill, and Finchley Road that she usually frequented.

Sometime later, relations between Mons and Eva seemed to enter a new, more serene phase, and she, apparently tired of her wearisome life as a night-errant model, devoted more and more time to her love for photography, shut away in her room in Camden Town. On many nights Mons missed her but accepted creative passion as his rival. He even encouraged it. He showed Eva's work to some gallery owners: photographs of chairs and strange bundles tied with cord. The Sunday photographer, he called her, because it was on weekends that she usually isolated herself in the Camden Town room that had no phone. On Shrove Tuesday, since she hadn't come back, he went to Camden Lock and after forcing the door and passing through a complicated network of ropes that crisscrossed the room in every direction like a chaotic spider web, he found Eva Lalka in the arms of a muscular black whose likeness Mons had already drawn by hearsay, both of them dead from an overdose of heroin. It was difficult to move in the room because of the ropes, and the lovers lying on a pallet on the floor seemed caught in the webbing. Beside Eva, on the floor, was a book entitled *Pornography*. The least pornographic of novels, I told Mons. *Pornography* is actually the name of the series of drawings by Mons in which Gombrowicz's book appears on the bed, on a night table, open and facedown on the floor, in a variety of frankly pornographic scenes that have Eva and the muscular black model as the only actors. In some she is photographing herself and her lover in complicated poses. In others she seems to be a store window mannequin, inexpressive, or perhaps inanimate, in the black man's arms.

I also recalled the painting of the contortionist wearing a white mesh costume so tight she looks naked, in a tense posture like a table, her head back, her hair brushing the floor, a poodle balancing on two legs on her pubis, all of it viewed through a fiery hoop by a clown voyeur. Mons titled it simply *Price,* and I suggested, because I caught the allusion, *Ara Maxima.* His stepsister, Ara, used to take him and his brother to the Price Circus in Madrid. There is a photograph of Mons at the age of ten, holding the hand of Ara, a slim blond adolescent, and standing beside a poodle. Whose name was Price, Mons said. In that painting named for a circus and a poodle, the red nails on the contortionist's hands and feet, firmly planted on the ground, glisten like drops of blood. Ara also polished her toenails, Mons recalled, and as a boy he admired his stepsister's meticulous brush strokes as she twisted into the most difficult postures.

Ara was a friend and confidante of Edmonde. In the early sixties they both performed in an avant-garde Belgian dance company. Mons painted them in *XX. Two Friends Dancing:* Ara the blond in a slit white dress spreads her arms and legs in an X next to dark Edmonde in an identical dress—but black—and pose, like a shadow figure. Ara was with them in Enfer when Edmonde committed suicide. Since then, Mons declared, he hasn't seen his stepsister. But he didn't explain why. And I didn't dare to dig deeper.

Another painting with a ghost from Mons's past: the

mature but svelte woman, her face and body painted in white-and-red geometrical designs (two Ms or mountain peaks superimposed on her left temple) who supports her conical breasts in her open palms and admires herself in a wall mirror, where she appears multiplied in multiple masks: a Luba mask with concentric circles around large eyes, resembling the head of Mademoiselle Pogany by Brancuşi; dark and pointed with a long nose like an arrow; smooth and lacquered, a smiling geisha; scowling with thick red lips and large white tusks . . . *The Woman of a Thousand Faces* is the title of the painting, and it is the only name Mons gives to the woman who was his second wife for a few months in London in the early sixties, not long after the death of Edmonde. I know that the mountain peaks on her temple correspond to the initials of her name. And her dress boutique. But Mons refused to say more about her. She isn't dead, he said, she's forgotten. Forgotten? One would have to decipher the significance of each mask . . .

*Pornography* could also have been the name given, perhaps with more etymological accuracy, to the series he chooses to call *Women of My Life,* one in every port, whom he has been drawing and painting from life on his many travels over the years. During his attacks of wanderlust, compulsion, or lunacy, in moments of crisis, even of panic. Almost running away, his instinctive reaction, not really knowing where. He likes to play what he calls "destiny roulette" and "airport roulette." When he gets an overwhelming urge to travel to the most unlikely spots. He goes with almost no luggage to the nearest airport, looks at the list of departures, one two three, the first name that comes up is his next destination. Which is why I received so many notes and drawings on hotel stationery from the most improbable places: "The view from my window, looking toward Penha Hill," he wrote from Macao a long time ago at the bottom of an ink drawing of ascending tiled roofs and flat roofs, laundry hanging from clotheslines, and signs with Chinese characters. When I looked more closely, I could see on a distant rooftop the tiny figure of a naked woman, like a Chinese character, raising her arms to a line that held undergarments. In another drawing sent sometime later from Buenos Aires, he repeated the game of a naked figure on a distant rooftop: "The view on this early December morning from the top of Calle Corrientes." Mons the voyeur . . . And only three months ago, from the Sicilian island of Panarea, he sent me, on the stationery of a Hotel Raya, nothing but a line—a *raya*—of blue ink that depicted perfectly the marine horizon he must have seen from the terrace of his room. In reality a hotel room in any city at all is, for a few days, his best studio, better suited to his restless nature than his permanent workroom in Berlin or Enfer.

I know he also sends travel notes and sketches, some of them quite daring, to a confidante and old friend, the silent friend, he calls her, an Italian marquise who breeds horses near Enfer.

Another recipient of his travel notes and studies, a Swiss collector, is a woman who loves the nomadic hotel life as much as he does.

On occasion Mons's passion for prostitutes, his Muses, combines with his passion for museums. That's why I suggested he lengthen the title of his series: *Women of My Life and Art.* Art, he told me, is part of life.

The weary Indonesian in black bra and panties who

yawns and raises her hands behind her in her small, red-lit display window is viewed from the street, among the silhouettes of curious onlookers, by a strange, resplendent, rather large-headed blond girl who has just stepped out of Rembrandt's *Night Watch*. She is one of his *dames* of Amsterdam.

The redhead clad only in her hair—it covers her right breast—and red stockings sits with legs spread wide on a three-legged stool and opens with curiosity or care a white package, perhaps a handkerchief, beside a table that holds a white porcelain vase of irises. The painting is entitled simply *Rachel,* and the real model was a prostitute in New York whom Mons met shortly after admiring van Gogh's flowers in the Metropolitan Museum of Art. He also depicted her in a red raincoat, her face made up like a geisha's, in the painting called *Dame de Sixth Avenue.*

*The Phantom of Battery Park* is the title of another strange oil that shows a nocturnal view of a ghostly, illuminated Statue of Liberty in the distance, while in the foreground a couple copulates against a parapet overlooking the water. The woman's raincoat is raised, and her legs are wrapped around the waist of a man wearing a dark suit and hat. She has black hollows for eyes and heavily painted lips. The man is kissing or biting her on the neck. A little to their right, a partially visible fisherman stands beside his rod and seems to ignore the scene.

It's true she resembles Eva Lalka. A little while ago, in Berlin, Mons told me about a strange encounter two or three years earlier in New York. One pleasant night or midnight in April, he was contemplating the bay and the brightly lit ferries from Battery Park and chatting from time to time with the night fishermen, when Eva's ghost appeared. He saw her approach a Japanese fisherman, some distance from him, who shook his head several times. Was he declining her services? When she silently approached Mons, he thought he was hallucinating. He had impulsively left too noisy an opening at a studio between Church Street and Broadway and gone for a walk to clear his head, but apparently he hadn't walked far enough. The cool sea breeze did not dispel the vision. She wasn't wearing anything under the raincoat, Mons insisted. The painting may reflect what a deluded Mons did or thought he did. The woman's legs are almost as white as her raised raincoat.

Mons's attraction to streetwalkers and brothel scenes stems as much from his nomadic life as from his somewhat romantic identification with certain artists, such as Toulouse-Lautrec or Degas, who belong to the same bordello fraternity, or "brothelhood," one might say, and transformed the women in that life into art.

There is a large painting by Mons, divided into several paintings, like an irregular checkerboard with a few black squares, that is ambiguously titled *The Adventures of a Young Model* and is especially intriguing; I would venture to guess that for the painter it was a kind of catharsis. In the distinct paintings within the painting the same dark woman appears, with curly hair, a ringlet on her forehead, almost like a question mark, and a rather triangular face that has a charming cleft chin. She stands nude on a circular platform covered with a tapestry, her slippers by her feet, surrounded by clay statues that represent her more or less faithfully. On April 1, 1976, in Paris (I recall the date because we were together in a taxi when we heard the news of Max Ernst's death), as we were driving along the rue du Dragon, Mons told me that his mother had worked as an artist's model at the Académie Julian in the early thirties, before she was a fashion model. Mons said that when she was very young she had run away from home with an actor who abandoned her a short while later in Paris. Her lover was the image of Rudolph Valentino, and she wasted no time in cultivating a resemblance to Pola Negri. She led a truly adventurous life in Paris (certainly a scandalous one for a girl from a respectable Madrilenian family) before returning to the fold with a son and marrying the Belgian businessman who could have been her father as well as the adoptive father to that boy of unknown paternity. Though I've seen only the portraits Mons recently did in Baden-Baden of a fairly dry and austere lady, simply entitled *The Widow I, II,* and so on, I suspect she is the young model in the multiple painting, perhaps as Mons pictured her in his disquieting fantasies and hypotheses. She also appears naked in another square in the painting, lifting her hands to the back of her neck, half seated (sitting only on her left buttock while her right knee touches the floor) on a chair covered by a white towel, while an anonymous hand holding a pencil sketches her in a notebook. And she appears as a model drawn by Erté, with art deco decorations and lines, wearing a variety of outfits from the 1930s. The most resplendent is cut out in the back in an almost Brancuşian row of large rhomboids, and she wears a matching necklace of rhomboidal jet beads. Even more startling is her presence in a fresco in an oval room: the nude brunette with the ringlet on her forehead lifts her right hand to her left breast and raises her right leg to dance in a garden with other women, who are naked under filmy veils and linked by garlands of flowers. I asked Mons if he had been inspired by Matisse's *La*

*Danse,* and he replied by nothing but *la joie de vivre.* And she is smiling as she lies on a deck chair beside the railing of an ocean liner and a life preserver that reads S.S. PROVENCE. LE HAVRE. The railing and the bright blue sea are clearly decorative simulacra in a room that is meant to resemble a stateroom. She also appears lying nude, facedown on the skin of a lion with gaping jaws in a room adorned with African masks, spears, shields, and drums. And she is surely the woman in the third-to-last painting in the painting, sitting on a bidet with her back turned, reflected in the mirror of an armoire before which a man is knotting his tie, back turned and suspenders dangling. In the next-to-last square the young brunette, ringlet on her forehead, appears with the body and wings of a sphinx at the top of a column. The last square is black, and up close one can detect a curl or perhaps a black question mark.

The painting within the painting, and the voyeuristic impulse, also appear in the scene of the couple who copulate standing up (she on tiptoe with legs bent and separated in the ballet position called *plié de pointe*) and are spied on from the other side of a mirror without silver backing—it is framed like a painting—by a voyeur with the profile of the writer Louis-Ferdinand Céline. The painting is called *Des touches au 31, Cité d'Antin.* The title alludes both to the alloy and the painter's brush strokes. I was the one who told Mons that in a house of assignation located at that address in Paris, between the rue de Provence and the rue La Fayette, in the early thirties, Céline was witness, on the other side of night and a trick mirror, to the couplings of his friend Elisabeth Graig.

In the brothels of Mons there is above all the voyeuristic

eye, the passive passion of the obsessive observer, an impulse that undoubtedly drives Mons to tireless nocturnal rambles through the red-light districts in so many cities, preferably ports such as Amsterdam and Hamburg.

A roulette wheel and a revolver appear on a scrap of movie poster on the leprous wall against which an emaciated woman in a miniskirt is leaning in the painting called *Rue Saint-Denis*. And we spectators follow the game with our eyes, not sure we understand.

I recall that on a lunatic summer night in London, in the early seventies, at a party of artists—almost a circus troupe— in Islington, Mons insisted on bellowing, to the leaps and cries of the madmen around him, the story of Actaeon, the hunter who accidentally glimpsed the goddess Diana at her bath and was turned into a stag torn apart by his own dogs. The myth of the voyeur Actaeon would inspire an ironic self-portrait of Mons dressed as a hunter and sitting under the great branching antlers of a trophy hanging on the wall, shading his eyes with his hands and looking through two open, symmetrical doors at a naked blond who stands and washes herself in a tub surrounded by the painting's green background. The scene is near Richmond Wood, in the ground-floor apartment with garden where one of Mons's models, whose name really was Diana, lived. And she also appears, Mons explained to me, squatting naked in the posture of one of the "demoiselles d'Avignon" (a critic from *The Times* said she was defecating) in a view of the Thames with Tower Bridge in the background.

And there is, in my opinion, a connection between the brothel theme and Mons's still life of two yellow books—*La Joie de vivre* and *La Fille Elisa*—and an old five-franc coin at the edge of the table. Mons first called it—or synthesized it—*La Fille de joie*. He crossed out the title on the back of the canvas soon after completing the still life a few years ago in Berlin, and beneath it he wrote: *Van Gogh's Alms*. I'm not sure the second title is better. The painter Stock had recently told him, in the Café Strada in Berlin, the parable of the saintly van Gogh who, as payment for a seductive smile, gave a Parisian streetwalker near the Saint-Lazare station the miserable five francs he had just been paid for a painting, which was all the money he had, and continued on his way alone, his stomach empty but his heart full of virtue. Mons, however, wasn't very sure about the virtue of his picture and destroyed it a few nights later along with other "still lifes that deserve to be dead," as he put it.

There are erotic paintings and brothel scenes by Mons that also include a book with a clearly visible title. I am thinking in particular about the paintings of the snow-white nude in black hood and stockings who assumes lascivious poses near a night table (lit by a lamp in the form of a phallic mushroom) on which is prominently displayed a book bound in dull red cloth, the title in gold letters: THE SACRED FOVNT. Did the novel by Henry James have some symbolic or hidden function? I asked him. It was there, he said. And the V for the U in the title or delta of Venus? It was there, he cut me off. Several years before he finished chronicling or completing for me the story of his first well-paid portrait. In London, when he was in his early twenties and leading a difficult but carefree life with other members of the group that would eventually be called Artychoke. He was living at the time with Mel, the waitress of his love and a student at the St. Martin School of Fine Arts, and he would sometimes go with her and the Dutch painter Albert Alter to sketch portraits of tourists in Trafalgar Square and behind the National Portrait Gallery. Head-hunting, they called it. On a hot, humid afternoon early in July, when he was sweating smudged trickles of charcoal, he was lucky enough to sketch three or four tourists almost one after the other on the steps of St. Martin in the Fields. He was ready to pack up when he was approached by the truly strange, sickly-looking man who hadn't taken his eyes off him as he worked. Mons particularly noticed that in spite of the heat the man wore a long dark overcoat with a fur collar, white gloves, and a dark felt hat. He reminded him, Mons said, of a portrait of Diaghilev. Except that the stranger had a brutal face, a sallow complexion, and a goatee. And was bald, as Mons would see when they sat down in a pub on the corner, Lord Chandos, to discuss the proposed portrait. At first Mons understood that it would be a portrait of a woman, perhaps the stranger's wife or lover, since she was waiting for them in a room at the nearby Charing Cross Hotel, where they were staying. The stranger had a German or Austrian accent (Mons recalled that he said they were returning to Vienna the next day), and if he was satisfied with the portrait he would pay him on the spot, in dollars, a fee that would allow Mons to spend his longed-for year in New York. A moment before, in the pub, Mons had talked about his artistic ambitions. Poor fool, said Mons, I thought my future as a painter lay in New York. I would have been better off staying in London. In New York I learned nothing but tricks, gimmicks for climbing the greased pole, a thousand ways to seem new instead of being who I was. When the stranger mentioned the amount (never ask any less for a portrait, he said), Mons thought he was crazy or pulling his leg. He also believed it could be a stratagem of Mons Senior. The stranger might be someone sent by his adoptive father to help him out financially. He rejected the idea because Monsieur Mons liked to make his good deeds public. Or he might be someone sent by the anonymous progenitor he was always trying to imagine. When Mons walked into the room on the second floor of the Charing Cross Hotel with his unknown patron, he thought no one was there. The heavy red drapes on the windows were closed (later he would see that they faced the Strand) and there was only a sliver of light from the almost closed bathroom door. Which opened wide to reveal a dazzling sight: a naked woman, tall and slender, with an intensely white skin that contrasted with her black hood and stockings. Mons was stunned. The woman walked past him in silence and then went to the bed, on the other side of the room, and lit the lamp, covered with a cloth, that was on the night table. She stood quietly in the diffused reddish light, as if waiting for instructions. Mons confessed that a thousand hypotheses passed through his mind. What did they really want of him? The old lecher undoubtedly wanted him to make the most pornographic sketch possible (in the style of Rops?) of the hooded woman. Some Soho bird impersonating his phantoms? Mons was utterly mistaken. It was the old lecher who wanted his portrait painted by Mons. Then came the strangest part, and it was difficult for Mons to understand. The old man wanted to be portrayed not on paper, canvas, or panel but on the extremely white, soft skin of his wife's belly. On the night table there were tins of tinted inks and brushes and a red book, *The Sacred Fount*. The odor is what Mons remembers best, but it is indescribable. The woman's odor, said Mons, was that intense well-lubricated *odore di femmina,* combined with the smells of mud, of faint, sweetish putrefaction, perhaps of smoke and blood, and other more tenuous scents he could not identify. The old lecher, sitting in an armchair beside the bed, looked at him with bulging eyes and waited for him to begin. At first his hands were shaking, Mons admitted, but he had never painted with a hard-on before. What would Dürer have said . . . With each brush stroke he felt as if he were caressing the woman's belly and pubis. The hairs of the brush in her silky, almost albino pubic hair. He knelt for a moment and bent over her belly, painting, and when he looked up he caught a glimpse of the delicate cleft chin under the hood. Mons's passion for dimples . . . Could the woman be wearing a hangman's hood? The old lecher was pleased to see himself on the woman's belly, with his high forehead, large bloodshot eyes, sparse pointed beard, some-what prominent eyeteeth, lips slightly parted in satisfaction. One would say that in the portrait his nostrils flared, or per-haps it was a slight contraction of the naked belly . . .

Mons, completely disconcerted, ran out of the room as if the Devil were at his heels, but in his pocket was a bulky envelope full of dollars that were not counterfeit, as he would learn the next day, not far away, at the Royal Bank of Canada on Trafalgar Square. How many dollars? I asked him. Never believe a painter's figures, he said. He preferred to go on talking about the hooded woman. Incredibly white. Harder to paint than the old man with his sallow complex-ion. He planned to include her in his painting of paintings, *Mons Veneris.* The idea came to him one evening when he was riding in a train near Paris and saw a mountain of trash and detritus reflected upside down in a dark puddle. He wants to incorporate into that inverted mountain the erotic scenes, lovers, models, and fetishes of his life and his art. From the black stocking of his earliest masturbations in Madrid to his lucubrations over the hooded woman in London. The right canvas was waiting for him in Enfer, one that was too big for his studio in Berlin. When I began to ask about the masturbatory stocking, he said he preferred not to recount stock stories. *De haut en bas* . . . You'll see it all in *Mons Veneris*.

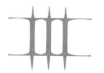

# Cézanne
# Ends in Anne

NGELUS NOVUS. Now that they're saying History is dead, her muse accompanies me. The only one who hasn't abandoned me? And finally she stops. A tranquil muse: *Muse mit Musse,* I muse. I park the Clio among the apple trees, and as I water them, whew, I wistfully regard Tübingen in the distance. Through these fields they would take the sainted poet Scardanelli out for a walk. A prairie prayer . . . It is the hour of the Angelus, and in the car I devour the remains of a leathery sandwich. The apple tree in front of me is heavy with black fruit. And suddenly, when I open the can of beer, the flock of blackbirds flies away. Now the timid sun peeks out and the bare branches of the apple tree cast a strange winged shadow on the ground.

*Annunciation.* (3–25–93) Today's the day. A date in Tübingen with Anne and Cézanne. The large black letters that spell CÉZANNE on the banner at the entrance to the Kunsthalle undulate and jostle one another in the wind, and I would swear at times there's an added H so that the billowing announcement says CHEZ ANNE. In her studio in Berlin Anne had a Cézanne poster that depicted a tall, luxuriant pine. A wink at her arboreal patronymic.

*Happy Ending.* I haven't seen her since she left Berlin a year and ten days ago. The Ides of March. Will we find one another changed? In my urgent letter—the day before

yesterday—asking her to meet me in Tübingen on the pretext of visiting the great Cézanne show here, I concluded
with a conclusive CÉZANNE ENDS IN ANNE. I didn't give her
time to respond: silence grants consent?

*The Cézanne Clinic.* I came directly to the Kunsthalle after
my snack on the outskirts of Tübingen. I had a hunch that
Anne would also come directly to be Cézannetized. To be
healed and made whole in Cézanne after more than a year
apart from art. (Beyond art there is no salvation?) In any
case, I left a phone message at the Hotel Krone. Please say
I'm waiting for her at the Cézanne clinic. At the dental clinic?
the receptionist asked, falling into the trap. An old game of
ours, because in Berlin Anne worked at a dental clinic that
we had transformed into the Cézanne clinic. Cézanne for
tooth, or *Zahn.* Anne moved from making dental prostheses
to shaping strange jaws of plaster and sharp nails at night
in our Steinplatz School of Fine Arts. Fraulein Pine and
Wooden Man soon became good friends. Another thing we
had in common: French mothers. Our studios were next to
each other, and she often came to mine—Klaus's cell—for a
drink and conversation. She talked more about family problems than artistic ones.

*Artists' Lives.* We also met frequently at the Filmbühne,
a café across from the school. And with other artists discovered the new dives open from dusk to dawn in the dilapidated buildings of Berlin Mitte. Together we descended—
the ascent was not so easy—into the dissolute depths of the
Caipirinha. And had our final drinks and straws at Friseur, a
former barbershop. That night Anne claimed that Mons was
cultivating a baldness à la Pollock and I a set of bangs like de
Kooning's. I found in her a resemblance to a Magdalene by

Perugino. The shape of her face really was the same, and she had the same pouting lower lip. But we couldn't always tempt her into joining us on our nocturnal rounds. Anne's practical theory at the time was that she had to choose between living her life or her art. The choice isn't always possible. Unexpectedly, that's life, she had to return to the Black Forest to manage the family hotel. Her father had suffered a stroke. What would I have done in her place? I recall my father's incredulous expression as he clutched at the counter with both hands when I told him of my intention to be an "artist." Did I know how artists lived? He had all the precision of a Swiss pharmacist: They live badly and die worse. If you don't believe me, just think about van Gogh.

*Cézanne Draws a Line.* Disheartened at not seeing her yet and at seeing the line that stretched around the corner of the street on which the museum was located. Philosophenweg. Philosophically I resigned myself to queuing in this cutting, almost wintry cold. And after so many hours on the road. Arctic for art's sake . . . it's clearly my way. And more and more pilgrims arriving. Busloads of schoolchildren and pensioners. Saint Cézanne in his sanctified, quantified shrine. I climbed up to the entrance and came down again even more slowly, peering into every face. She wasn't there. Suddenly I was sure she was waiting for me inside. I raced up the concrete steps and with a face of reinforced concrete slipped impassively past the penitents already at the portals of paradise.

*Birthday Present?* Black and violet on the white porcelain of the tank. This Chinese notebook (MADE IN CHONGQIN CHINA), its cardboard covers spattered in inkblots, found barely an hour ago in the WC of the Kunsthalle. Lined pages—still virgin. An early present. It's not till tomorrow. The age of the Passion. Ecce Pictor, as Mons says. So much precious time wasted! At my age, van Gogh had only four years left to finish his work. And Modigliani, three. And Walter Kurt Wiemken, none. That's life. In any case, I appreciate the present. The best proof is that I've already begun to use it, here in the museum cafeteria, as I wait for Anne in the shadow of the stone buttocks of this great reclining nymph. True repose in the smooth polished posterior as opposed to all the puckered chicken-ass mouths chomping on more and more sandwiches and pastries. Cézanne apple tart. Sainte-Victoire crullers . . . The multitude fed in the cafeteria. Well fed. Cézanne for every taste.

*Grosse Kiefer und rote Erde.* And you couldn't move in the exhibition rooms. I looked for her again in the impenetrable forest that obscured the view of Cézanne's trees. In the glass that covers *The Murder* (1867–1869) the reflected faces of the spectators look sinister. Two ruddy matrons and a bald man with a white goatee laugh in front of a still life with a sulking skull. Poor Yorick—To be or not Tübingen . . . And at last I knew Anne was there. Perhaps I saw with my pineal eye (that's how I'd explain it afterward) the great pine firmly rooted in red earth, vibrantly spreading its long branches to embrace the entire canvas. The great pine from the Hermitage in Saint Petersburg, which I saw so often in the poster tacked to the wall of Anne's studio in Berlin. Looking at the poster and joking about her last name, Kiefer, I once said to her: At least you know your family tree.

*Out of the Artistic Woods?* But I, Holzmann, what stuff am I made of? In honor of my name, "wood man," all my work in one way or the other, in substance or in theme, has to do with wood. Carvings, sculptures, paintings on wood, wood-cuts. The etchings in the series *Pinacotheca,* dedicated to Sansón Carrasco, Aurore Dupin, Peter Kien, Pinocchio . . . Or the totemic danse macabre: *Totemtanz.* So many tree trunks so carefully carved. Masks of men and animals, faces of wood, *gueules de bois,* jaws of pine, arms of branches, trunks of trunks. My Birnham Wood provisionally positioned in the interior courtyard of my house in Kreuzberg and sometimes used by the neighbors to hang their clotheslines. The spirit of the forest—and of Daedalus—is not always understood.

*Life Lines.* (An hour later.) I went back to the museum cafeteria to continue waiting for her. At last, and I made a move to get up, wrapped in a red raincoat and shaking wet hair off the back of her neck, in walked the woman I at first mistook for her. Anne's type—her good looks—but not her style. She pulled off her raincoat, and as she sat down at the next table I noticed the shadow cast on her cheek by the golden cluster of grapes dangling from her downstretched earlobe. A pendent pendant. They're not ripe . . . It's plain to see I'll remain alone. Just as well I brought the book of poems—my breviary—by the recluse of Tübingen. What an extraordinary coincidence has now brought together in this small city the greatest poet of Germany and the greatest painter of France. Cézanne was born four years before the death of Hölderlin, and both—for different reasons—spent most of their lives withdrawn from the world. They knew that true poets and artists are strangers in their own land. I decided here, near Cézanne, not to delay any longer my visit—for the first time—to Hölderlin's tower. What if Anne wanted to surprise me and was waiting for me there? She knows my passion for the poet. So many titles of my works were lines from Hölderlin *(Hölderlinien . . . )*. For example, the series *Life Lines.*

*The Other Half.* Other strangers in their adoptive land. Memorialized in graffiti painted on this wall of the university where bicycles are leaning. ASYLHETZE: ROSTOCK, BERLIN, MÖLLN. Cold silent ramparts. Are they going to trample him? Head and trunk of a Turk: at the entrance to the bridge the half man, cut across the middle, taps a tambourine, singing and giving thanks on the sidewalk. I went down to the river. Sitting on the parapet, groups of students dangle their legs over blue-tinged water. At the end of the promenade, on the banks of the Neckar, the house with the tower. Too yellow to be ivory.

*Fritz Hölderlin!*—sprayed in green along the yellow wall, like ivy growing rampant all the way to the door. I paid two marks to go in and lost all notion—all motion—of time in the tower. Like the mad poet Hölderlin, alias Scardanelli, who humbly signed poems dated twenty years before he was born. The small clavichord on the ground floor (it can't be touched or played?) let me hear the heartrending rasp of Scardanelli's long nails along the keyboard. And the flourish of a goose quill scratching on paper to the accompaniment of a rhythmic *rasgueado* . . . Did I imagine sobs as I climbed the narrow stairs? Apollo has pummeled me . . . would be the poet's piteous lament. No one but me in the tower. I would have liked to lean my forehead against the glass with Anne beside me so we both could see from this high window the scene seen every day by Scardanelli. A line of sheep on the small bridge transformed into a line from a poem. To draw and paint with lines from Hölderlin. In my head I have this painting: silver light on violet earth.

*Looking for Anne.* I was almost locked inside Hölderlin's tower, I should say the tower of the good carpenter Zimmer. He certainly had the right stuff to be Scardanelli's guardian angel. He and his family. Is there a Zimmerstrasse here? I got out just in time and wandered the streets of the old city. I leafed through books in a secondhand bookstore located in the house where—according to the plaque—Hermann Hesse lived from 1894 to 1899. He was also a painter. Of landscapes. Who's afraid of the Steppenwolf? Not this loner, who read I don't know how many times in Rorschach those notes meant only for madmen. Night was falling. I telephoned the Hotel Krone, to no avail. I drank beer in a crowded tavern named the Lichtenstein. At last I found the courage to call Anne's house in Bad Peterstal, but no one answered. I decided not to sleep in Tübingen, to go looking for Anne instead.

*Selva Oscura.* I recall as I left Tübingen the bright colors of male and female gymnasts circling, like fish in an aquarium, a high-ceilinged glass-walled room flooded with neon light in the middle of the night. I had planned to stop in Freudenstadt for something to eat, but the cold, deserted streets at that hour, nine o'clock, discouraged me. Resort towns, deserted as well, as I crossed the Black Forest. Lines of roads and mountain curves. Poles inserted at the edge of the highway. Clio breached the night with brush strokes of light. Forest sketches: Black lines and white specks on gray slate. Branches streak the bluish black, convulsed by the wind; crowns of trees still capped with snow shake loose the final clumps. Dripping to the rhythm of spring. In the night trees clash spectral spears: wood of the air. More darkened towns. And finally in this one, Griesbach, I was attracted by a smoky room where a forest of silhouettes was in motion. I looked in for a moment and ended up dancing the whole night with a nurse named Hortensia.

*Before Cézanne.* At last I reached Bad Peterstal, a little before noon, and saw the report in the paper. I cut it out to paste it here like an obituary:

### Fatal accident.

A 25-year-old woman, Fraulein Anne Kiefer, was killed yesterday afternoon at the wheel of her car on a secondary road that crosses the Black Forest north of Bad Antogast. For reasons that are unclear her Golf drove off the highway and crashed head-on into a tree. The unfortunate driver, who was alone in her vehicle, died instantly.

Was she on her way to Cézanne? Her life as brief as her art. Ideas of March: Take life as it comes. Gather ye rosebuds— not to mention Hortensia. Make no plans. April, May, and June are far away.

# Anne with Cézanne,
# or the
# Apple of Concord

You can look at it, said Klaus, if you haven't already . . . , and he burst into one of his strings of strangled hee-hee-hees when I told him on the phone that he had left his notebook at my place. No need to inquire at Exil, where we had eaten supper with Mons and Double Uwe the night before, or to ask Mons, in whose studio we'd had our next-to-last drinks. It's true Klaus had taken out his notebook in Exil: in the light of the billiard-table lamp he showed us the double-page drawing of a kind of schematic tree with bare branches and a wing-shaped shadow that he wants to transform into a sculpture, *Annexe,* in memory of Anne Kiefer. The last pages of the notebook were filled with drawings of trees, pines and firs in particular, in almost human shapes. Double Uwe suggested a video sculpture, the sound of the wind included, and I pointed out that the arboreal sculptures could be doubled if his drawings were employed as shadows on the wall. Klaus looked at Mons, no doubt expecting his comments, but Mons only asked that we speakers allow the sculptor to conceive his own artifact. Then Klaus said it ought to be a very restrained work, I recall he used these two words: naked and fragile. Like Anne? Mons seemed thoughtful, and back in his studio he asked Klaus to show him again the sketch of the pine that spreads its branches like the multiple arms of a Hindu god.

Anne brings us all to Cézanne, said Mons, and he turned around a large oil that was facing the wall, a painting taller than he which depicted Anne's empty studio in Steinplatz, the jaws of plaster and nails on the floor like the gaping maws of caymans and prehistoric monsters, and on the back wall nothing but the poster of Cézanne's great pine tree. At first glance a faithful copy of the poster. But if one looked more closely the reddish, whitish, greenish and bluish areas on the trunk and the first two aligned branches came to life in a surprising way: Anne crucified, Anne a dancer in an ecstatic pose, Anne in a trance, Anne as a dryad embedded in the great pine, the dark helmet of her hair partially covering her eyes, her slender body almost clay red as it was during her final summer when she sunbathed naked in the grass on the banks of that pond in the Grunewald.

I'll never be able to look at Cézanne's pine with the same eyes again, said Klaus, and his were wet with emotion and alcohol too, no doubt. I recalled that on my walks with Mons in the Grunewald, on the first afternoons of that almost Mediterranean September, we went to the Teufelsee because Anne was going to lie in the sun and swim there after she left the dental clinic in Dahlem where she worked a few hours a day. The Teufelsee, which Anne called "the Devil's pond" in French, the title of the novel her mother had given her to read on her summer vacation when she was thirteen or fourteen years old. Anne Kiefer with her Aurore Dupin, lying supine . . .

We looked for her in the meadow, the two of us fully dressed among the undressed.

A towel over her face, but I recognized her small conical breasts.

A terra-cotta figurine, Mons called her, and she really had taken on the color of red clay. Perhaps that was when the idea came to Mons of naked Adams and Eves who look like earthenware idols.

The two of us sitting on the grass next to Anne, sitting there naked, and I asked her to bring her right hand to her chin to complete the *tableau vivant*. Mons, however, asked her to pose for him sometime. Visibly gratified by the flattery, and perhaps to hide it, she dived back into the water.

Anne disconcerted, Mons recalled, when he stared so fixedly at her naked body. And intimidated too, I thought. She wasn't familiar with the Mons method of painting nudes. What he calls incorporating the body instead of copying it. Only when he has it sketched inside, in his gut, as he says, does he begin to paint. Often without the model present. The first time they posed for him, many women thought he wasn't a painter but a mere voyeur. In front of the model, woman or man—though his male nudes are in fairly short supply—Mons would sit, fist under chin, and do nothing but look for a very long time. Which sometimes felt to Anne like an eternity.

Anne standing, naked, lifting her hands to the back of her neck; Anne the Bather, squatting, lying facedown, kneeling, leaning forward . . . in fourteen paintings and postures of the fourteen bathers in *Les Grandes Baigneuses* by Cézanne in the Philadelphia Museum of Art.

And that other, disquieting canvas: Anne in black tennis shoes and white socks and nothing else, sitting sideways, her legs hanging over the arm of a rustic wooden chair. In her hands she holds a bowl, lost in thought as she considers (globs of plaster gleam in her short, mahogany-brown hair) the gaping jaws of the monsters at her feet.

I was one of the very few people privileged to see these nudes. Just in time, because soon after the death of Anne, Mons destroyed them. They didn't do justice to Anne, was his only explanation. At least we still have (for the moment?) the most mysterious one: Anne's pine tree. It had to be a pine—her doom and destiny, her sign and symbol—that Anne crashed into in the Forest as Black as her fate.

One afternoon Mons, Klaus, and I walked with Anne for hours in the Grunewald. And sat on the old pine log at a bend in the path that Mons dubbed "Kafka's log" after I told him Kafka used to rest on one like it during his walks through the Grunewald. On another afternoon Mons and I walked with Anne from Teufelsee to the nearby Teufelsberg. The Devil's mountain I call "Mount Mons" because he invariably passed by there on his Grunewaldian meanderings or meditations. Ruinous mountain, I called it, because it actually had been built from the ruins left in Berlin by the war, but especially because Mons anthropomorphized it into something monstrous or diabolical. That black, pointed shape, like a menacing shadow, seemed to pursue Anne in her nightmares after she saw it in Mons's studio. Yet Anne's mandibular creatures, bristling with barbs, were not precisely angelic. Mons bought one, a kind of beak with the teeth and neck of an archaeopteryx, about to take flight over a ledge of sharp-edged stones. It was called simply *Rock*, and Klaus referred to Anne's almost ornithological or oracular passion for observing the flight of birds. A species of space . . . not in space but made of space, she said one night in Filmbühne when they were commenting on the swift silhouette of a bird by Brancuşi. And I recalled that the street where I lived in Berlin, Storkwinkel, stork's corner, had inspired Anne and me to make some ambiguous jokes. Our remembrance of Anne, dead almost a year, was abruptly interrupted by the arrival of other happybirthdaying night owls. Mons seemed disconcerted. Who had spread the news that it was his birthday? Double Uwe's body shook as he hiccuped his hypothesis. And tried to convince Mons. When you're born on February 29, you have to celebrate on the twenty-eighth if it's not a leap year. He might have found support in Lichtenberg and said that someone who celebrates his birthday every four years is not like other people. Uwe was determined to celebrate it. Which explained his having invited us to Exil even though it wasn't Saturday. Double Uwe eats there almost every Saturday, always at the same table in the back, in the billiard room. This Viennese restaurant in Kreuzberg, on the banks of the not-at-all-Danubean-blue canal, calms his nostalgic appetite for the dishes prepared by his Austrian mother. The fillet he usually consumes, the *Tafelspitz*, we call *Tafelspitzel*, adding on a German spy, or *Spitzel*. A private joke that Klaus didn't know about. When Double Uwe goes to Madrid, the first thing he does is have lunch or supper at Horcher, the Austrian restaurant near the Retiro. Horcher, a good name: the spy, the one who listens behind doors; appropriately enough, Double Uwe always orders "fillet of spy," unless he's tempted by a Viennese *Schnitzel* that makes his mouth water and brings tears to his eyes. When we left Exil, Double Uwe suggested accompanying Mons to his studio. We didn't know then that he had the party all arranged.

Petra, Mons's model, came in, her hair dyed blue with

nails-like-talons to match, escorted by a Russian painter with the dark silhouette of a dancer from the Bolshoi or an ice-skater, and raven tresses à la Gogol, a recent arrival from Moscow who brandished a bottle of vodka as an offering. The English architect from the studio downstairs, Margaret the Iron-and-Glass Maiden, was accompanied by an elegant old man, the architect Ziegel, whom I took at first for a funeral home employee who had come to the wrong address, and as a present she brought a book of drawings of futuristic cities that drew an enthusiastic thank-you from Mons—Antonio Sant'Elia's *Città Nuova!*—the title echoed in a chorus of Italian by a married couple, both of them architects, he an Italian and she a Croatian, who looked like twin gray lumps of fat.

It's the real thing, the Croatian repeated in Italian with each glass of Russian vodka poured for her or that she poured for herself, with increasing frequency. And to completely fill the studio with smoke and personalities, the painter Stock arrived clutching his pipe, zigzagging and coughing, followed by the lame sculptor Frieda, swaying suggestively, and her new boyfriend, pale as a corpse and dressed in strict mourning, who's a photographer, I heard, along with part of his name, Andreas von Something-ending-in-off.

When the alcohol was flowing freely and Petra had begun one of her trance dances (for the moment she limited herself to lifting her short black leather skirt and showing off her black net stockings with oval holes at the knees and calves), and in view of the fact that Mons was growing increasingly impatient (his left leg rose and fell, almost pedaling, faster and faster, as he sat on the only arm of the one-armed divan, snorting out the smoke of his cigarette), I made my getaway with the excuse that I had an interview early the next morning. Klaus followed my lead and had the courtesy (or cunning) to offer to take me home. Don't trammel the Trabant.

As we approached Storkwinkelgasse, my street of ill repute, I told Klaus, recalling the appellation applied to it by Anne.

When he saw the Cadillacs embedded in blocks of concrete in the center of Rathenauplatz, he said they made him sick. Fake funerary stele . . . I believe he muttered between his teeth in French. Funeral cars, he added, bending his head even lower over the wheel. The wolf's lair, and he gave his nervous little laugh as he braked. I thought he was referring to the tavern on the corner, Wolf's Inn, its horrible white wolf's head still lit up over the door, where we had brought Anne one night, almost by force. I preferred not to bend my elbow with Klaus to imbibe the bitter beer of old haunts, and I suggested he come up to my place for a nightcap.

We sat face to face at the kitchen table, sipping grappa, and he lost no time in talking to me about Anne. The first anniversary of her death was approaching, and Klaus again took out the notebook with the preliminary sketches for the commemorative sculpture he was planning. He hadn't found Anne in Tübingen, he said, only the notebook . . . He had been so certain of seeing her that he had asked his sister for the Clio to make the trip. His sister, who works in a laboratory in Basel, had come to spend a few days in Berlin, and Klaus had lent her his studio in exchange for the car. It was a surprise trip; he let himself be carried away by a sudden impulse. Perhaps if he had arrived in Tübingen a little earlier . . .

If I committed the indiscretion of looking through his Tübingen diary before he authorized me to do so, it was because I was convinced he hadn't really forgotten it but only pretended to so that he could go on talking to me about Anne with greater knowledge on my part, particularly with regard to his feelings for her. And he probably wanted to show me that he had the stuff of a poet and had not been bragging when he told Mons and me one night, in the bar and library of the hotel on Fasanenstrasse—another street with a bird's name—that he had wanted to be a poet long before he turned to sculpture. I also saw that he wanted to sound me out regarding the artistic relationship between Mons and Anne. He suspected, I believe with reason, that it was not purely artistic. At least at a certain point. I especially recalled the night when Klaus went slipping and sliding after Anne through the snow on Yorckstrasse, asking her to stay with him. But Anne strode decisively toward our group— Mons, the painter Pi, Frieda, and I were a little ahead of them, looking for a taxi. When we had finished supper at Publique, we said good-bye to them at the door because Klaus said he would take Anne home. But we know that Anne, for once, did not want to go straight back to her room. Klaus left, his old jalopy—and his plans—backfiring.

Anne accompanied us on our nocturnal rounds, more and more insecure at each stop, and at the last one, Meyhane, our Turkish café on Kantstrasse, I realized she'd had more to drink than usual. Frieda and Pi didn't come with us after Rost, that narrow rusty bar on Knesebeckstrasse.

We're not oxidized yet, and Anne laughed, resting her head on the shoulder of Mons, who held her up by the waist. On Savignyplatz we took a cab. First we would drop Mons off at the Hotel Askanischer Hof, which was close by, and I would continue on with Anne to Witzlebenstrasse, just a step from my house. We were squeezed together in the backseat, and for a moment I thought Anne was crying against Mons's shoulder, but she was only laughing. That night Mons joked about the sculptures Anne had just exhibited, along with other students, in the great lobby of the Steinplatz School of Fine Arts. Particularly a phallic serpent by Anne, so opportunely placed it seemed about to be fellated by an enormous red tongue, almost the size of a bullock's, that moved in and out of a glass case, the work of another ingenious sculptor studying at the school. When Mons got out of the taxi, I was only half-surprised when she followed him. I watched them disappear, reeling arm in arm, through the door of the hotel. I wouldn't be going, then, to Witzleben. A name, long live wit, that does lend itself to jokes.

When I returned the notebook to Klaus two or three days later, I didn't have the courage to tell him that when he had traveled to Tübingen to see Anne with Cézanne, she had arranged to see Mons in Baden-Baden but canceled the trip at the last moment. She had spoken to Mons on the phone, very depressed because her father had suffered a relapse. Paralyzed and paralyzing her, according to Mons . . .

The following year, at the FIAC in Paris, coinciding with the great Cézanne retrospective at the Grand Palais, Uwe Wach presented a kind of offering to Saint Cézanne that included Mons's portrait or ex-voto, *Saint Cézanne*, with halo and some apples, perhaps by Gauguin; the oil painting of

Anne's studio with the poster of Cézanne's pine; and an early work by Anne herself: a little mutilated plaster statue of an armless Eros, with painted plaster apples and pears that appeared to be rotten. But the pears and apples that really drew the attention of visitors were the ones by Klaus—enormous, of polychromatic wood, some more than a meter high.

We saw each other a good deal during the fair in Paris, and I did an interview with him in which he spoke like a geometrician about his monstrous apples, and about Cézanne. He made short shrift of the supposed universal acceptance of Cézanne, who had been transformed into the beloved papa of all painters, even the least artistic newspapers and magazines gushing Cézanne, front and back.

On the resplendent morning when we rode together in a taxi to the Grand Palais, a trivial incident gave me the title for the article I was going to write about the Cézanne exhibit. As we were crossing the Place de la Concorde, a box of produce fell out of the van in front of us, and a single yellow apple—it looked like gold—began to roll across the square and between the wheels of the cars, dodging all of them, until it was lost from view. Klaus said this was one more proof of the saintliness of Cézanne.

When we were at the exhibition, standing before the *Quatre Baigneuses* with the magnificent *demoiselle* in the center who lifts her hands to the back of her neck, we heard an older gentleman say to a well-dressed woman of his own age, "The man couldn't draw; he's worse than Picasso." We both burst into laughter. At the time the blasphemy must have seemed like healthy dissent to us.

We stood in front of the great pine and saw Anne again,

as a dryad, and Klaus noticed that the number of the painting, 154, corresponded to the date of Anne's birth: the fifteenth of April. Anne boasted of having been born during the so-called Prague Spring. The blue serenity of the portrait of Madame Cézanne made me see again, I don't know why, Anne in the Grunewald. Perhaps Klaus was thinking of another Hortensia . . . He continued talking to me about Anne in the brasserie across from the Grand Palais. Looking at the menu, among the sorbets and ice creams, we couldn't ignore "La coupe Cézanne." But best of all, Klaus pointed out, was "La coupe Picaso," with only one *s*. Just as well it didn't say Picoso, or pockmarked.

Didn't Anne have a few freckles across her cheekbones? Again I saw her oval face, the face of the Magdalene by Perugino, the cleft chin so carefully detailed by Mons.

Anne's pine was everywhere, on the poster for the exhibition and on the cover of the catalogue. Klaus said he could see himself two years earlier in Tübingen, in front of the great pine, when he had the premonition that Anne was there. I wanted to show him that I had carefully read and translated his travel diary, and I said the last sentence was a line from Hölderlin. April, May, and June are far away, Klaus recited in German. Did he mean to suggest that he was prepared to pass on to the next line: And I no longer want to live? Klaus closed his eyes for a moment, as if blinded by the sun, and stared absently at the poster on the glass door gleaming with Anne's pine.

# The Architect's
# Destiny

IEGEL the architect speaks as if he were elsewhere about his extraordinary cities and buildings, while Mons, who gives more credit to what he sees or thinks he sees than to what he hears in his dilapidated Berlin studio in Kreuzberg, continues to move from plane to plane with translucent overlapping strokes of the palette knife, representing and reconstructing Ziegel in a full-length portrait in which he wears rigorous black like a clergyman but sits with somewhat awkward informality on a riser of a spiral staircase, his right hand like a claw clenching a thick, closed yellow book on his right knee, his back against a high wall of yellowish bricks, or books perhaps, as light touches of the brush refine the lines but do not lessen the decrepitude of his sunken chest and cheeks or the labyrinth of wrinkles on his long ashen face where a pair of steely eyes intermittently flashes behind his glasses as he evokes certain spires and ogives. Ziegel has visited so many cities over the course of so many years that his memories are beginning to fade, and at times isolated details are all that are left for him to hold on to. These details—from his staircase Ziegel had just evoked roofs bathed in blood, perhaps by the setting sun— and other trivial reminiscences were the real souvenirs of his distant travels. And on occasion his recollections over-lapped, one city duplicating another, doubling in this way the duplicity of memory. But Ziegel does not forget that in the long run memory is one of the names we give to imagination. When he walked through a strange city he sometimes suffered the strangeness of déjà vu. Where had he previously seen the rose-colored tower of Margar under a blue sky, facing the arcaded plaza with its equestrian statue? And the palaces of brimstone, with ashen colonnades and statues, in ruins at the edge of blue-black waves, or the spectral nocturnal cities of the guests of stone, funerary statues as silent as the grave, where petrified factions and putrefactions phosphoresce among sarcophagi, peristyles, rotundae, stelae, and skeletons? On occasion, with an effort at concentration that further wrinkled his sempiternally scowling brow, he managed to place precisely where he had previously seen those streets and alleys, those disquieting labyrinths that he believed he was walking for the first time. Which is what happened to him when he visited the place called the City of the Immortals.

That delirious architecture seemed to spring from the opium visions of De Quincey and Coleridge, semisymmetries in a chaotic kaleidoscope where dromedary domes rose beneath the cupola of night, mad truncated caracole staircases against unsalvageable walls, lofty basalt rising over the abyss, pilasters soaring to the stars and splintered plinths and prostrate rostrate columns, the sharp beaked peaks of their rostrums earthbound, and alligators astride astragals in the black sun of melancholy. Inaccessible windows, bottomless pits, unimaginable chasms, and no less unimaginable upside-down staircases with inverted steps and banisters—Ziegel saw them all again in the inextricable prisons of Piranesi cor-

rected and augmented in the visual paradoxes and conflic-
tive perspectives of Escher's etchings.

Ziegel could also see in the moonlight the countless
columns, duplicated by their shadows, that rose almost to
the clouds and whose capitals, in an unknown style of architecture, served as a refuge for nocturnal birds scrabbling
the heights like raptors among the skyscrapers of Miami
before descending the interminable marble staircase that led
step by step to the abyss of subterranean fire in the palace
composed of an endless succession of immense rooms,
of columns and arcades that converged in a luminous point
like a sun about to be consumed on the horizon. No less
oppressive for Ziegel was the vast constructed nature—that
was how he described it—of the kingdom of Arnheim,
designed, almost dreamed, by the American millionaire
Ellison, emulator of the extravagant English millionaire Wil-
liam Beckford, with its sinuous canals, its hills covered by
luxuriant vegetation artistically arranged over the landscape
(which, according to Mons, the Belgian painter Ensor had
varnished with sun and gold dust), its amphitheater of purplish mountains opening to the vast splendor of groves,
lakes, meadows, streams unfolding before Arabigothic architecture almost suspended in the air that makes the projec-
tions, oriels, minarets, and towers of filigree and gold gleam
in the purple sun of twilight. Ziegel believed he was looking
at the Xanadu of Kubla Khan and Mr. Kane. But he not only
found enchanted houses that seemed to float in perpetual
levitation. He saw others, no less formidable in appearance,
that collapsed suddenly in a thundering whirlwind of dust.
Like the diseased house of the diseased Roderick Usher, with

moss-gray walls and lugubrious Gothic towers, when the scar that zigzagged the length of its facade began to open.

He experienced a comparable atmosphere of decadence, though terror gave way to tedium, when he visited Fontenay-aux-Roses, near Paris, the retreat of the esthete Jean des Esseintes. He recalled, above all, the study whose walls were lined in Morocco leather, the Latin books on ebony shelves, the parquet floor covered with the skins of leopards and blue foxes. He advanced, one might say, contrariwise. Against the grain. What especially caught his eye was an enormous live tortoise on an Oriental carpet, a myriad of multicolored precious gems encrusted in its shell. In fact, he probably did not pass beyond the suffocating foyer, overflowing with so many ostentatiously artificial flowers and plants that they seemed more real than real, more real than luxuriant nature. The natural plants imitated the artificial ones to perfection, with leaves and corollas that looked like tin, like glazed cloth, like starched calico . . .

One would have thought the house-cum-museum of decadent horrors had been decorated by the count of Montesquiou. Or by the baron of Charlus.

He never had a greater sensation of unreality than when he visited the house of the writer Pierre Loti in Rochefort, and walked through rooms of different periods and cultures, a potpourri of exotica: the red nineteenth-century salon with its portraits of ancestors, the Turkish smoking room, the mosque, the library of mummies, the Gothic sitting room, the Renaissance dining room . . . until he reached the austerity of a stark whitewashed room, the cell of a warrior-monk if not for all the brushes and combs coquettishly arranged on a small table. A gram of madness, of *folie,* really, he said to himself, to counteract the Huguenot severity and right-angled design of Rochefort.

At times Ziegel believed he saw himself reflected in a nineteenth-century painting, *The Architect's Dream,* by his compatriot Thomas Cole, which he had seen many years before in the museum in Toledo, Ohio, and which depicts a man in a red tunic reclining atop a colossal column and contemplating a magnificent panorama of pyramids, Parthenons, coliseums, and Palladian palaces.

The mysterious atmosphere prefigures certain surrealistic works and some metaphysical architecture by De Chirico. For an architect, Ziegel believed, what matters is the purity of a dream, the purity of line in arcades, towers, terraces, columns.

The mystery and melancholy of a street, its arcades stretching to the horizon, and the child who chases her hoop along the deserted street toward the human shadow emerging from the dark building on the right: he has experienced this in various cities. As well as the joys and enigmas of a strange hour in a strange city.

He had heard of the existence of a city with multiple names, perhaps at the edge of a desert, a city entirely constructed of blocks of yellowish stone called the stones of destiny. Engraved on each stone is the story of a life, sad or happy, that can be deciphered only by the traveler who recognizes himself there.

Beneath the icy circle of the full moon and beyond a thin veil of mist there appeared to him on the snow-covered slope of a mountain the fine black lace silhouette of the city of Getulia that seemed to come from Paul Klee's *Book of Cities*.

To better remember his interminable journey through the fifty-three cities of the country of invisible symmetries, which form a parallelogram composed of four isosceles triangles and have women's names (who said that cities are women?), Ziegel constructed an alphabetical atlas, from Adelma to Zoë, which confuses the chronology and will confuse it again at random in the memories of the painter Mons (he particularly recalled Perintia, the city of monsters), who listens as he paints Ziegel on an autumn afternoon in Berlin, for the traveler who disembarks in Adelma will recognize all the inhabitants who cross his path and eventually will recognize himself, poor mortal, resolving at last the enigma of his arrival; it is easy to lose one's way along the concentric canals of Anastasia; in Andria one can orient oneself on its streets by following the order of the constellations; in Argia, however, the streets do not look to the sky but bury themselves along with their houses, which are filled to the roofs with clay; Armila is a city without houses, though it does have elevated water pipes crowned with sinks, bathtubs, and showers, where the nymphs who are its inhabitants merrily wash and bathe; Baucis is a city one never sees because it is suspended high in the clouds; and from his staircase Ziegel added that at times the roles are reversed and it is the traveler in the clouds who can barely make out the tiny city hugging the earth far below. Mons believed he understood the full extent of this remark a few weeks later, in the Café Einstein, after reading FATAL FALL in the *Berliner Morgenpost*: Ziegel fell or threw himself into the void from an office building under construction on Potsdamer Platz, and the article completed his curriculum vitae by stating that the American scholar and architect of German origin Peter Ziegel, author of a biography of the English architect James Wyatt and of the *Book of Imaginary Architecture,* had taken part, during the Second World War, in the bombing of Dresden.

Perhaps the imaginary cities that so obsessed him could not completely erase the blazing real city razed by fire from the air, and innumerable fictional buildings could not delay his arrival at the final real tower of the final gamble in the final house of his final destiny.

On the desk in his office, like a paperweight on top of the tower of documents, a ragged anthology of Rilke in which this line from "The House" was carefully marked in pencil:

> Another terrible fall

Ziegel was profoundly intrigued by a tower, mentioned by Chesterton, whose architecture is, in and of itself, perverse. Did he ever find it? The banality of evil dispersed among countless low-income housing projects and labyrinthine shanty towns of concrete and abominable beehives?

In one of his earliest memories, Ziegel, enveloped in a silvery gray fog, watched in terror as a house came alive—its window a bulging eye, its door a wide-open mouth—until it was transformed into an ogre. Perhaps it was in a darkened movie theater,* he told Mons, who then amplified the vision by explaining to Ziegel that the entrance to the concentra-

---

* Ziegel's vision probably originates in an animated sequence from the 1907 American film *The Haunted Hotel.*

tion camp at Auschwitz, painted in perfectly realistic fashion with its two windows and door, looked like a devouring ogre in *If Not, Not,* a painting by R. B. Kitaj in the Edinburgh Museum of Modern Art.

And Ziegel in turn explained to Mons, complicating the vision for him, that the demon in Dante's *Inferno* appears as a building and a machine, a kind of diabolus ex infernal machina, a sort of giant windmill—poor Don Quixote!—raising with his batwing vanes the winds that freeze the soul.

Ziegel's *Book of Imaginary Architecture,* included in Mons's portrait of him, has exactly 410 pages, no doubt in order to fit on one of the twenty shelves in one of the innumerable hexagons in the Library of Babel. But in that vertiginous universe and architecture the book and the city—*byblos* and Byblos—will become one and the same.

# The White Lady
# of the Métropole

T HE white lady of the Métropole, Mons called her, a startling apparition he attributed to his high fever and anti-flu rum (it only made him high) when he returned in the small hours to the Hôtel Métropole in Brussels. After staggering through the marble splendor of the lobby to the long counter in the rear to ask for the key to his room and turning left on his way to the elevator, Mons said, holding himself as stiffly as he could, an apparition?: the hooded lady in a white cloak who seemed to be sleeping peacefully, sprawled in a chair against the corridor wall just between the recessed column and the sparkling showcase of perfume bottles, he reported in detail, her arms outstretched and her hands—in white cloth gloves—lying open on a small table with slender curved legs. (Her life raft, really, as he would soon discover.)

As he passed through the forest of potted palms and Corinthian columns in the bar, which was empty at that hour, he could not control a sneeze, he recalled, so loud he turned to make a gesture of apology, but the lady or mannequin (could she be a decoy?) remained motionless in her seat. What was she doing there at that time of night . . . Suppose she was dead, he wondered finally when he was in bed. On All Souls' Night . . . Or had she simply fallen asleep waiting for someone or coming home from a party after a little too much to drink? His sleep was disturbed by incongruous nightmares. The thunder resounding against the wall startled him awake. It's not possible! And Mons confessed that he jumped out of bed, indignant. When he arrived the previous night he was given a room, or rather an echo chamber, adjoining a discotheque, and the rock-and-rollicking roar kept him awake. His room had been changed but not, it seems or sounds, the noise. He dressed, determined to make a scene at the reception desk. Or was the noise coming from downstairs, from the bar? The hotel bar, in fact, was open again, enlivened by a gathering. Of misogynists? At a bachelor party? More than twenty gentlemen in evening clothes, most of a certain age, all with mustaches and some with white beards, who actually seemed to have come from a wedding. Only one lady among them, also in dark clothes, fortyish, her hair pulled back in a chignon. The lady, who reminded Mons of someone he couldn't quite identify, sat on a leather couch between two solemn-looking bearded men, raising her left hand to her left ear and turning in the direction of a medieval suit of armor that clubbed or rather hammered at the grand piano where, leaning on his elbows and listening attentively, there stood a young man with a dark mustache and unruly hair who resembled Albert Einstein. Suddenly the suit of armor struck the keyboard with a tremendous blow of his mace, a clamorous finale that sent keys flying through the air, and extended his iron hand to the young man with the wild hair of a scholar. When he bent forward as if to kiss the gauntlet, it turned red hot, and Mons awoke, he asserted, with scorched lips.

It did not take him long to realize that scholars had filtered into his dream (Einstein, Madame Curie, Max Planck,

Poincaré, among others he could not recall) from a 1911 photograph that hung across from the reception desk of the hotel and had immediately attracted his attention, reminding him that on the mantel over the fireplace in the library of his grandfather, Dr. Verdugo, there was a picture of Madame Curie with her hand at her ear. The Deaf Woman, as he called her when he was a boy, had reappeared in his dream.

Had he dreamed the white lady too?

The next night, back from another artists' festivacchanalia* that had a good number of toasts, he found her again, sitting at her little table in the hotel corridor in almost the same pose, wearing a turban and a long pearl-colored silk dress that seemed to come from a fashion magazine of the 1930s or a theatrical wardrobe. Could she be an actress? A very pale face, he thought at first it was powdered white, eyes and brows lightly emphasized, and black like her hair, which the turban did not cover completely. Delicate lips, tightened into a scarlet line. A cleft—the touch of Venus, Mons calls it—in her chin. He also noticed the slenderness of her legs, the mother-of-pearl gleam of her silk stockings, the pointed toes of her slippers. The figure of a fashion model, that's how Mons planned to draw her, a *Vogue* fashion model from the old days, or from the time of Paul Poiret, though of indeterminate age, perhaps a well-preserved sixty. And Mons did not ignore her left hand, also gloved in white and holding

---

* In a troglodytic bistro behind the Hôpital Saint-Pierre, whose Flemish name sounded to Mons like "Au steak-à-pattes," which is how he sketched it in his notebook, a fillet-centipede or "scallopendra" [sic] so difficult to cut they had to shout for an Aztec knife instead of the "couteau-à-steak."

to her ear a small radio that barely emitted a hum or faint cooing. Could she have fallen asleep listening to the radio? Or, in order to fall asleep and not feel lonely, did she need the bill and coo of the transistor-turtledove?

Mons the night owl saw the sleeping white lady again on other occasions, always in the elegant clothes of a lady from another time, as he made his way to the elevator.

He was eating supper one night with a colorful group of Belgian friends when he mentioned the strange case of the *dame* of the Métropole. There were interpretations for every taste, which Mons annotated and illustrated in his notebook. A professor of Spanish literature at the Free University of Brussels said half jokingly, half seriously, that she might be a *dama-duende,* the ghost of a guest at the hotel who, for reasons that escaped him—and he smiled maliciously at Mons—only he was privileged to see. A homeopath ("a pathetic Romeopath," according to Mons) favored a therapy of hypnosis-induced amnesia at the place and time of the event the patient could not remember. An actress of the Kantor school said it might be a kind of happening with an ending as yet unknown. And, since it was closing time at Vincent, he proposed continuing the false hypotheses in Le Falstaff. A Belle Époque decor for the *belle dame de l'époque* . . . And the poet—Flemish—of the group, who was also a music critic, added with ethilyrical exaltation and conviction that she was the beautiful Irina, a Russian Pavlovian ballerina, a has-been defector who led a nomadic existence in the cities of her earlier triumphs, and that the Métropole was her refuge on the nights she spent in Brussels. Instead of ballerina, write down a former model for Balenciaga and Balmain, said a gallery owner who was an expert in haute

couture and collected seascapes and landscapes by the
designer Poiret. (He probably was not aware that Mons's
mother, using the somewhat shortened name of Carmen
Verdoux, had been a model in Paris in the 1930s.) Mons had
also considered and discarded many other no less lunatic
hypotheses, but he was convinced that reality really is or
becomes stranger than fiction.

Finally he decided to ask.

Madame Mayer? The man at reception seemed uncom-
fortable as he pretended he couldn't find or was looking in
pigeonholes for the key and the explanation. Almost in his
ear, he whispered that she was Swiss, one of our oldest
clients, just think, she stayed here for the first time when she
was seven or eight years old, and lowering his voice even
more he informed him that as a result of a fire in her house
she suffered crises of anguish and claustrophobia at night;
considering these exceptional circumstances and the fact
that Madame Mayer would soon be leaving for another hotel
in another city, for she was a great traveler, the hotel man-
agement allowed her to sit discreetly in a corridor, always on
the ground floor and near the entrance, because of her fear
of a possible fire, until daybreak gave her enough confidence
to return to her room, where a hot bath, drawn by a chambermaid, awaited her. After her bath, and breakfast in bed,
Madame Mayer, surrounded by her latest acquisitions, for
she was an *amateur d'art,* rested for a few hours. This is what
she did, day after day and night after night, until the crisis
passed.

The story seemed so extraordinary to Mons—and surely
he was energized by the white lady being an *amateur d'art*—
that in his room that same morning, tired of watching the

rain fall on a wet place de Brouckère, he drew from memory several sketches of the white lady asleep in her chair, her somnambulist's arms extended toward the little table. He also made separate paintings of certain details in the Hôtel Métropole: candelabra with twisted arms, clusters of globular lights, chandeliers multiplied in mirrors, gilded columns, stylitic sphinxes with gilded angel wings and the faces of women on the high, blue glass windows of the reception area, sirens who hold aloft or proffer heraldic coats of arms from the great lamp in the café of the hotel, caned chairs and round tables on the café terrace reddened by electric heaters beneath the red awning and in front of the plaque that reads THE MÉTROPOLE HOTEL in gilded letters, perspectives of arcades and arches with coffered ceilings, palm fronds against plinths, high doors between embedded marble columns, somewhat threadbare reddish carpets with intricate traceries on floors of salmon-pink marble, the art deco spiral of a staircase like a superposing of octagonal gems, a bellboy in scarlet jacket and cap and black trousers who looked like a puppet by Goya retouched by Ensor . . . , without supposing—or so he claimed—that in a few days all those sketches would adorn, like ex-votos, the chamber-chapel of the white lady in the Hôtel Métropole.

Truthfully, who was she?

Rosa Mir! exclaimed Vanderdecker, the great Belgian collector, when Mons asked him on the phone if he knew Madame Mayer. Rosa Mir, a prodigy on the violin and a no less prodigal collector, a legendary character long before she became Madame Mayer and especially after she was widowed in tragic circumstances. She had married one of the founders of the Swiss pharmaceutical firm Gebrüder Mayer; or both of them, Vanderdecker explained maliciously, because the brothers were inseparable twins, at least until the fire that caused the death of the one married to Rosa Mir. Who was Spanish, didn't he know? And he had the idea of giving a dinner party at his house in honor of this most extraordinary collector so that Mons would have the opportunity of seeing her awake. And he did. The striking lady in white with a white feather boa (the white widow? a way of wearing negative mourning, like the Japanese?) inspecting with the air of Sherlock Holmes or Maigret a Magritte (a monstrous red rose that filled an entire room) and frowning so much that Mons told himself she was going to exclaim, "This is not a Magritte!" Or, even worse, "This is not a rose!"; but she only murmured in French, "In the good old days I had the white one," at least that's what Mons believed he heard as he stood next to her in a secluded hallway lined with half a dozen Magrittes. *Dans le bon vieux temps?* "Yes, the white rose called *Le Tombeau des butteurs,*" she said and pointed to the title on the frame of the red one: *Le Tombeau des lutteurs. The Tomb of the Fighters* was an enigmatic title, but *The Tomb of the Earthmounders,* what a word, may have been more appropriate for a rose in the form of a colossal cabbage that blanches when it is buried . . . Mons knew nothing about earthmounders or *"butteurs"* and was about to ask how it was she no longer had the Magritte of the white rose, when Vanderdecker interrupted or intervened to make introductions.

(And he could not have imagined at the time that not long afterward he would plan, in homage to this Rosa

Mirabilis, to plant in her room at the Métropole an enormous white rose like a captive globe that would keep growing alicecarrolly while in the distance a violin plays and the
voice of Jacques Brel resounds:

*Rosa rosa rosam*
*Rosae rosae rosa*
*Rosae rosae rosas*
*Rosarum rosis rosis*

And as the broken record told the beads of its rosary of
roses, after all a rose is a rose ad infinitum, the monstrous
white rose would keep growing and overgrowing to the
crashing crescendo of a sobbing violin in the living or dying
painting called *Le Tombeau des luthiers*.

Strummer of coffins cum laude, does every encrypted
rose have its thorns?)

With their host they reviewed some masterpieces dis-
tributed with casual discretion throughout his residence.
Difficult to imagine that this duplex on the avenue de la
Renaissance, in a modern building with a bland facade,
housed such jewels. A soaring Tower of Babel raised its
ochers and golds behind a black writing table. Madame
Mayer or Rosa Mir let escape, in Spanish, an *Ay, mi Memling!*
that came from her soul as she bent over the diminutive dip-
tych, open like a small illuminated book on the black table: a
Nativity with two blue angels, the one on the left playing a
lute, the one on the right a bowed *vihuela*. Not exactly her
Memling, but it did bring back painful memories. Vanderdecker kept guiding her, delicately and affectionately, toward

the stairs that led down to the dining room. Mons had the good fortune, thanks to Vanderdecker's foresight, to eat at the same table as Madame Mayer, or simply Rosa, as he would eventually call her. Earlier, at the beginning of the meal, he had been surprised when she did not remove her eternal gloves or plumed serpent. Mons deduced that she must have suffered burns on her hands and—since he noticed she always kept it covered as well—her neck. Perhaps the painter regarded her then as one of his *Têtes brûlées* and tried to catch a glimpse of her burns. *Nécrose trémière?* . . . Vanderdecker had already told her about Mons's monstruaries and in his country house south of Brussels had shown her some recently acquired pictures—from the series *Shrunken Heads* and *Goyatine*—that had made a profound impression on her. In that macabre "tête-à-tête gallery," as one critic called it in *The Independent* of London, Mons had tried to settle the score—a spiteful poke in the eye, perhaps—with certain art critics, dealers, and one or two colleagues. She had been particularly horrified by a large bearded head—belonging to a midget Holofernes?—partially wrapped in a sheet of bloodstained newspaper. Head of critic on critical background . . . Do we Spaniards always have to be cruel? she asked herself and him as they moved into the adjoining drawing room to have their coffee. Always violent? Mons, who perhaps was only half Spanish, spoke to her then of the *calme*—and *luxe*—that favored the *volupté* of volutes, as they were enveloped in the whorls rising from a Havana cigar that had just been lit near them by a powerfullypaunchyplenipotentiary, and he alluded to his lovely sketches of the Métropole, somewhat faded testimonials to a once glorious past, in which she demonstrated a lively interest and asked that he show them to her in the hotel the following day. Bring all of them! she ordered.

They returned to the hotel together after midnight in Vanderdecker's limousine, driven by a chauffeur whose skull was as clean-shaven as Mons's and who had—a detail that did not escape the attention of the creator of *Primo Carnera Boxes with His Own Shadow*—cauliflower ears, as did so many boxers. Speaking of the noble art, Rosa Mir tried to describe a picture in her collection—it had added fuel to the fire— that was attributed to George Bellows and depicted an extremely elongated bald black boxer, all arms and legs (Jack Johnson? Mons wondered), who with his outstretched right arm held back in the ring a line of white zombies leaning toward him, or perhaps a single zombie coming at him in a series of successive positions and deconstructions of move- ment in the style of photographs by Muybridge. A Bellows combat with a Balla kinetic touch, truly unique.

When they reached place de Brouckère, Mons thought he heard her call him Hadrian. Though she, fortunately, did not seem aware of the lapse. After swirling like a whirlwind through the revolving door of the hotel and striding reso- lutely to the reception desk, she announced cheerfully, key in hand, that tonight she was not on guard duty and was pre- pared to spend it oh-so-comfortably in her bed of roses. The euphoric effect of champagne? Or of Mons's company?

Mons was convinced she was inviting him to follow her ipso facto (fatuous?) to her room, but he thought it more prudent to wait until the next morning.

He appeared punctually at a quarter past eleven with his portfolio of métropolesque sketches, and she received him in elegant dress, lacy fichus worthy of Beardsley at her throat and neckline, and led him with utmost care into her personal bazaar so crowded with furniture, pictures, sculptures, books, bibelots, and all sorts of odd-looking *objets* that he could barely take another step. Mons recalled a series of works of unequivocal Belgian character, which the collector Rosa Mir had surely acquired in her expeditions through the galleries and studios of Brussels.

A sculpture in steel and black marble (a casserole of shellfish, *Brussels's Mussels,* signed Moulaert) on the dresser beside an open box of Godiva bonbons in which, instead of "Princesse noire," "Palet d'or," or "Manon blanc" . . . there was a selection of glass eyes. On the left, next to the window, a display mannequin in a felt hat and a stole in the style of those worn by Rosa Mir was engaged in reading *Le Soir* at a small round table on which there was a bottle of Mort Subite beer, a glass with an imprint of red lips on the rim, a paperback novel by Simenon entitled *La Chambre bleue,* a pack of cigarettes (which reproduced inside a small circle the head and hat of the reader of *Le Soir*), and a yellow box of matches with three red torches on it.

On the opposite wall, in a life-size portrait, a false Negro or minstrel in blackface displayed his white teeth and held in his raised left hand a round black and gray box of blacking, brand name ÇA-VA-SEUL.

On the night table, under a glass cheese cover, and at the edge of the daring décolletage of two painted hemispheres, a fan of cards (clubs, hearts, diamonds) with the ace of hearts showing. In a corner a dedication written in pencil: "To Madame Mir, a token of friendship," and an illegible signature, apparently in Cyrillic characters. As he leaned over to examine the signature—Vladimir? Valdemar?—Mons observed that written beneath the central heart of the ace card was the brand name CARTA MUNDI.

Rosa Mir appeared impatient to see the sketches and pointed to the bed—the only space that seemed to be free—so that Mons could display them. A new patchwork quilt began to spread across the counterpane. Observing how she looked at the polychromatic details of the Métropole, Mons realized that her eyes strayed in a curious strabismus: the right one, the fixed, hard eye of a bird of prey, glared with determination, cupidity, and calculation; but the left, damp with emotion, reflected only love of art.

That was the essential image of Rosa Mir retained by Mons in the anamorphotic portrait *Imago Mundi,* in which the collector, with many artifacts at her feet, looks with straying eyes at a globe of the world (which turns out to be a lute lying belly-up) and an oblique compass rose that is transformed (a Holbeinian wink) into a skull. In the deformation of perspective, Rosa Mir's extremely elongated neck and her head with its chignon are, if one looks carefully, an inverted violin.

The collector Rosa Mir appreciated the selected fragments of the Métropole and the wealth of details but missed one that was truly significant and important to her: the monogram formed by the entwined letters HM on the glass at the entrance to the hotel, which from a distance look like a golden butterfly. They were also the initials of her late husband, Hadrian Mayer, and of his favorite painter, Hans Memling. The butterfly is a symbol of resurrection, isn't it? . . . To her mind, in fact, Hadrian continued in some way in this world—in her world of an itinerant collector—and she wrote to him almost every day, recounting her travels and encounters and new acquisitions in detailed reports, just as she had when he would send her to the most remote corners of the globe in search of new pieces for his art collection. A generous collection that brought together primitive and modern art and built bridges between ancient and contemporary masters. Hadrian also had an eagle eye for discovering embryonic genius. She would not dispense with his astute judgment. She sent her letters to a Polish clairvoyante in London who had once been painted by no less a figure than Kokoschka and who transmitted her husband's responses back to her. And on the little Louis XV table on which she rested her hands when she slept, Rosa Mir indicated several bulky envelopes addressed to Madame Starzinsky in South Kensington.

Madame Starzinsky also sent her extraordinary automatic drawings by a very young English painter who had committed suicide in the late 1920s because of a fatal woman named Dolores, a model for the sculptor Epstein. They were extremely expressive drawings, faces for the most part, and it was at a show in London of these portraits from beyond the grave where, in an act of Providence, she met the clairvoyante. After that transfigured night, as she called it, said Mons, she had become a convinced spiritualist. From time to time Madame Starzinsky would also send her the intriguing conversations Hadrian Mayer held with Chang and Eng, the famous Siamese twins of the last century. Rosa Mir picked up the bulky envelopes with their Hôtel Métropole imprint and said it was preferable to deliver them by hand because she had decided that within forty-eight hours she would be in London. If any ideas occurred to him for decorating her room at the Charing Cross Hotel, she told Mons, she would be there for two weeks. When he was in London her husband had always stayed at that hotel, through which several generations of Mayers had passed since the turn of the century.

Mons might have revealed to her that his first commissioned portrait—a most uncommon commission—had been completed in the antiquated hotel that was almost on the skids. He didn't, why should he, and said to himself: She's a little crazy . . . and might have repeated it in French and Italian to underscore the artistic hodgepodge in her room at the Métropole. Mons admitted he could not have imagined at the time how contagious the manias and extravagances of Rosa Mir were and how much they would inflame his creative fervor.

Rosa Mir paid him generously for the color renderings of the Métropole, but in a few days Mons was painting for her two Siamese men dressed very formally in frock coats and watch chains, their arms around one another's shoulders like good brothers. Was it an affectionate embrace or a wrestling hold? The Siamese on the right has a somewhat contorted neck, partially open mouth, glassy eyes. It also looks as if he is tipsy and his brother is holding him up. According to Mons, the painter cannot allow himself to betray a confidence, to interpret. He was fascinated by the story of the Siamese twins transformed into a circus spectacle, and by their Dr. Jekyll and Mr. Hyde qualities. Chang was short-tempered and frequently drunk, while Eng was sober and affable. In 1843, when they were thirty-two years old, they married two American sisters, Adelaide and Sarah Yates, and managed to maintain separate households by rigorously alternating, three days with each wife and taking the seventh as a day of rest, as God commands. The system must have worked because each one fathered several children. Mons also painted the two sisters who had married the Siamese twins, arm in arm and wearing identical red shawls, as in *Les Deux Soeurs,* the canvas by Chassériau in the Louvre, Mons explained to Rosa Mir, which was painted in the same year as the marriage of the Siamese twins to the Yates sisters. Mons, who was almost as obsessed with twins as Dr. Mengele, proposed painting a series of double portraits or double figures. Perhaps he had in mind the Mayer twins and their collection or *Gemäldegalerie.*

For years following their meeting in Brussels, Mons kept appointments with Rosa Mir in hotels all over the world, or—when he could not travel—sent her works intended to distract the collector in the solitude of her gallery hopping.

Mons kept a recent article, folded and refolded many times, from *La Vanguardia* of Barcelona; it was a complete curriculum vitae.

### Rosa Mir
### Worldwide Collector

Rosa Mir, the widow Mayer, a nomadic native of Barcelona who even as a child, in the 1940s, traveled the world as a violin prodigy in a meteoric career that was mysteriously interrupted at the age of thirteen after she won first prize on the New York radio program *Rising Musical Stars,* is still a tireless traveler and a no less extraordinary collector and patron of art. In 1982, following the tragic death of her husband, the Swiss chemist and collector Hadrian Mayer, in a fire at their villa "Vieux Temps," on Lake Zurich, when he attempted to save some of the masterpieces in his collection of contemporary painting, Rosa Mir decided to carry the torch and bear witness, so to speak, to his burning passion for amassing art and supporting artists, in a totally original way that would reflect her tastes and character: she is a compulsive collector. According to an article in the *Neue Zürcher Zeitung* a few days after the fatal blaze, Rosa Mir stood before the still smoking ruins of the villa from which she made a miraculous escape and determined never again to have a home as she had in the good "vieux temps," or to have no more than a home for the day. She would live only in hotels, changing cities frequently as she had in her years as a violinist. When she learned that the priceless collection of paintings and no less valuable furnishings—the article made special mention of a secretary with secret drawers crafted by Roentgen—had been almost totally reduced to ashes, Rosa Mir told the *Neue Zürcher Zeitung* she decided to set up "nonpermanent," or transitory, collections, for just a few days, in the hotel rooms she would occupy. In reality, the Swiss newspaper declared, her only permanent possession was a small Louis XV table of the type called "cabriolet" and signed by Dubois—that was the crux of the matter—which saved her life when she held it over her head as she left the burning villa, protecting herself from falling red-hot metal and thus fulfilling the prediction of the antiquarian in Geneva who had claimed when he sold it to her—believing it was all a joke—that touching Dubois brought good luck. The table accompanied her in her wanderings from hotel to hotel, during many insomniac nights. And so Rosa Mir became "Compass Rose" to her friends, an indefatigable roving collector. Often when she arrived at a new hotel, the paintings, drawings, and sculptures, the wide variety of objects she had commissioned from artists and friends, would already be waiting for her. She also tirelessly visited the principal galleries, antique stores, and artists' studios in each city, looking for new pieces. When the hotel room became so crowded she had the feeling there was no more room, even for her, she resigned herself to a change of scene and began her "nonpermanent" collection all over again in another city. Then she would ask her friend Carles Taché, the Barcelona gallery owner, to empty out the crowded room and distribute the works to other collectors. In

reality, Rosa Mir confessed, her collector's
passion was satisfied by acquiring an extraordinary piece and keeping it only for a short
time, like fishermen who are satisfied with
the thrill of the catch and return the fish to
water before they go.

Each hotel room occupied by Rosa Mir
became a kind of *cabinet d'amateur* and, at
the same time, without her realizing or
desiring it, a sui generis installation.

On occasion the works collected or
requested of artists by Rosa Mir had a the-
matic character, which heightened their
resemblance to an installation. For example,
she filled Suite 79 at the Hotel Imperial in
Vienna with violin cases opened like strange
butterflies or coffins in which dolls lay
wrapped like mummies, perhaps a mysterious allusion to some event in her past
as a violinist. The most provocative piece
was a work by the young Austrian sculptor
Strunk, reminiscent of Duchamp: a violin
bow lying across the bidet in the bathroom
of the suite. In a room at the Gramercy Park
Hotel in New York, she re-created an "interior" by Roy Lichtenstein, with an identical
sofa, carpet, and lamp, and the great American artist came personally to hang the missing portrait of Mickey Mouse. She filled a
room at the Hôtel Lutétia in Paris with
books about rooms in several languages:

*Voyage autour de ma chambre* by Xavier de Maistre, the Spanish edition of *A Room of One's Own* by Virginia Woolf, *The Enormous Room* by e.e. cummings, *Room at the Top* by John Braine, *Röda rummet* by August Strindberg, *Le Mystère de la chambre jaune* by Gaston Leroux, *Chambre d'hôtel* by Colette, and many others, illustrated with drawings by friends who were artists residing in Paris. In the Hotel Askanischer Hof in Berlin (which she prefers to the more luxurious Kempinski because Kafka used to stay in a hotel of the same name, though in a different locale and no longer in existence), the young Swiss sculptor Klaus Holzmann filled her room with a multitude of wooden figurines in the most absurd postures, which he entitled *Kafkaballet*. The portfolio *Imago Mundi*, which the painter Victor Mons has just presented in Barcelona, gathers together many anecdotes regarding the life and miracles of Rosa Mir, her marvelous world, her trip around the world in eighty hotel rooms—number 204 in the Hotel Majestic of her native Barcelona could not be omitted—and her passion for errant collecting.

Shortly after the publication of this article, Mons returned to Brussels and from the Hôtel Métropole wrote a strange letter to Rosa Mir at the Hotel Majestic in Barcelona:

*Compass Rose:*
*They tell me you've just left for Barcelona. What bad luck!*
*We passed each other en route. I'll have to paint you as the*
*"Maja of the Majestic." Another time . . . I'm remembering*
*the good times. Soon I'll paint for you the portraits of your*
*favorite violinists, beginning with Henri Vieuxtemps and*
*not forgetting Ingres or Sherlock Holmes. Unless you prefer*
*Ralph Holmes. Speaking of detectives, I have to tell you the*
*most mind-boggling piece of gossip you've ever heard. The*
*day before yesterday I met Storiani in Geneva, at the bar in*
*the Hôtel des Bergues, and he told me—don't fall down!*
*hold on tight!—he assured me—but he had already had too*
*much to drink—that you were not you, that's just what he*
*said, but everybody knows Storiani always speaks badly of*
*other collectors and mistrusts them, and he said you were*
*an actress or former actress hired by Rosa Mir to play her in*
*all the hotels of the world. This is certainly a Storiani story!*
*And the real Rosa Mir was so horribly disfigured in the*
*fire in her house that she lives as a recluse in a new lakeside*
*villa on the far side of the Léman, a villa with neo-Gothic-*
*Moorish towers inspired by Gaudí, appropriately called "La*
*Stravaganza," never leaving, never letting anyone see her,*
*not even her brother-in-law Horst Mayer, who lives under*
*the same roof. She is always veiled, or hooded, according to*
*some versions, and dressed in black. And she has set aside*
*certain chambers where one can communicate with her only*
*through jalousies like those in cloistered convents. Storiani*
*went on with his story. He claimed that the surviving*
*Mayer brother is so devoted to his poor disfigured sister-in-*
*law that he allows her this comedy of the double—her nega-*
*tive, one might say—and the manias of her collecting and*

*her spiritualism. Of course I treated Storiani the histrionic storyteller as a joke, and my laughter frightened away the last remaining barflies. I can imagine the good laugh it will give you. Will I see you soon? At the Lutétia?*

*Painting you with love,*

And on a separate sheet—of music—he had drawn the aquiline profile and willful chin of a man playing the violin and had written at the bottom: Don't you think Huberman's profile resembles Holmes?

Mons finally decided to send her the drawing but not the letter. In the event Storiani's mad story about the madness of Madame Mayer, or all the Mayers, caused her pain and made her relive particularly painful memories. Rosa Mir has been somewhat depressed recently, said Mons, and is suffering again from insomnia.

# Paris as Paradise

ONS painted him as *A Pilgrim in Paris:* a volumi-
nous black silhouette holding a staff and wearing
a cloak covered in Santiago de Compostela scal-
lop shells, who raises his head—topped off by a Sherlock-
holmesian cap—toward a Cubist Eiffel Tower that explodes
into prisms of every color. A strange pilgrim of truly singular aspect . . .

The peregrinations of Reck in Paris at the end of June
1994, and the zigzag of his restless mind, are meticulously
recorded in his cramped microwriting in Joyce's notebook,
that is to say, in the notebook that Joyce, his wife, bought for
him at the National Portrait Gallery in London, which has
on its cover a reproduction of a portrait in oils of the writer
James Joyce, who stands, arms folded, holding a cigarette
in his right hand and leaning against a table covered with
books, his eyes glancing left. He wears an olive drab suit, a
gray vest, and a really splendid tie with specks of yellow, red,
black, blue . . . When one looks at it closely—Joyce pointed
out to him—it becomes a black man or a clown in a beret.

It was her final gift to him, given on an afternoon the previous June when they had taken shelter, during a sudden
downpour, in the National Portrait Gallery, in the corner
with a large window near the portrait of James Joyce she
liked so much. That was when she showed him the figure or

background of the tie. She had the fairly well hidden whims of a painter and an imaginative eye, but even so he was amazed she still had the heart to notice such details only hours after it was confirmed for them—she always insisted on knowing—in a gloomy north London hospital that her death sign was cancer. She died a few months later in Providence, Rhode Island, on the morning of January 6, as Pilar and Robert Coover, our mutual friends, informed me. Thanks to the Recks—who were still in London—I was able to interview the writers Robert Coover and John Hawkes in Providence for the last installment of a piece on New England that Mons illustrated with Lovecraft's long face and the elongated shadows of extraterrestrial monsters.

All the books by Professor Frank M. Reck—and all of them deal with Joyce—are dedicated "To Joyce." The critic Julio Ortega, Reck's colleague at Brown University, pointed out with his usual perspicacity that the dedication was a doubly equivocal allusion, one riding the back of the other. (Saddling the beast with two backs . . . the irreverent habitués of Nighttown in *Ulysses* would add.) The fact is that Reck had been a husband for as many years as he had been a specialist in the Irish writer.

Speaking of dedications, I remember the one he wrote for me in French, playing with my name, in his extremely involved book on *Finnegans Wake:* "To Emil, night and fog for nyctalopes." A short time before we had talked about *Providence,* the Resnais film whose title he considered deceptive.

I hadn't seen him since 1990 at the James Joyce symposium in Monaco, where I had delivered a paper called "Place Your Bets!" (I can still see him in the casino at Monte Carlo, paying more attention to a crane in a fresco than to the spin of the roulette wheel and then refusing to gamble with a categorical couplet: From Monte Carlo I went without betting a cent . . . ), and our next encounter, at the entrance to the Law School in Seville under a punitive sun, was preceded by doubts until he, stately and plump, raised his arms in a ritual gesture, invoking the resemblance I had attributed to him when we met for the first time at the symposium in Dublin in 1982. But he no longer had the abbatial air of the majestic Mulligan, the false curate and apprentice cure-all who, holding aloft a bowl at the top of the Martello Tower, opens the introito to *Ulysses*. He was heftier, he had grown his little Oliver Hardy mustache, and in his dark clothes and black tie he had the mournful silhouette of Leopold Bloom.

For some time Reck had been preparing an exhaustive study of Joycean epiphanies, *Epiphanies Without End,* its impending publication perpetually postponed, as if to pay homage to the title, and in the bus that carried us to an estate on the outskirts of Seville where the Bloomsday supper was to be held, I informed him with relief that finally, at my insistence, the edition of Joyce's epiphanies illustrated by our friend Victor Mons would finally be published—and in Germany. This book too, in a series of setbacks, had suffered considerable delays. About ten years ago, if I'm not mistaken, I had met with Mons in a room at a small hotel in the Latin Quarter in Paris, on the rue des Carmes, where I generally stayed in the early eighties, to examine the texts and probable problems in illustrating an edition of the *Epiphanies* that would incorporate the latest discoveries deciphered in the labyrinthine manuscripts at the James Joyce Archives. Paris was a feast of epiphanies, I recall, which we prolonged in a nearby Lebanese restaurant and, after midnight, with new libations and deliberations at the Café Le Métro on the place Maubert. I keep as souvenirs some sketches Mons made with a flying pen in that café—on cardboard coasters with beer advertisements—as I read selected epiphanies to him, what an eye, eh! he emphasized, what a wizard's eye! with strokes of his pen: a wave that pounces like a feline, sad figures of half goats in fields of thistles, a strange mangy bear or monkey splashing in a puddle, a spider shining in the inky night like a star . . .

As the bus drove through the fields of Seville, I asked Reck if the title of his book, *Epiphanies Without End,* indicated that throughout his life Joyce had done nothing but write epiphanies. Wait till you see the final judgment, and he gave me a wink. (I didn't know yet the state of his study.) And then I saw, in the seat in front of us, a woman from the conference wearing a carnation in her gray hair like the Andalusian girls recalled nostalgically by Molly Bloom.

A few days later, when he arrived in Paris, Professor Reck may have had difficulty finding lodging and fortunately recalled the quiet hotel on the rue des Carmes that I had mentioned to him.

A small hotel, as I had told him, but the elevator seemed like a coffin to him, so narrow he almost had an attack of claustrophobia. He also had some initial doubts about the cleanliness of the room (on the second floor, across from the old convent—of the "brown scapulars," he noted— on the rue des Carmes) because in the corner between the toilet bowl and the wall of the stall shower he found, lying facedown—or covers up—a slim volume, bound in white cloth, of the poems of Ungaretti in a bilingual Italian-

German edition published by Suhrkamp. A confirmed bibliophile accustomed to bibliographical precision, he also noted that the translator was Ingeborg Bachmann and that it was a second edition, dated 1966, in good condition though the jacket was missing. But first he picked up the book and looked at and let himself be dazzled by the first poem, "Mattina":

M'illumino
d'immenso

It was an epiphanic moment of sudden illumination. Reck, invariably Joycentric, added that Joyce would have said: I am illuminated by the insignificant. The particular is what really counts. The detail. Always enlightening. "Illuminations and Eliminations," in fact, was the title of one of the densest chapters in *Epiphanies Without End*. Rimbaud and his voltaic rainbows, as well as the short circuits of the mystic poets and the lightning flashes of haiku, were well known to him, but until that moment he had never read anything by Ungaretti.

He continued reading and rereading aloud, in Italian and in German, lying on the bed, until twilight, when his belly began to rumble, wreaking even more havoc on his discordant Tuscan tones. German, on the other hand, was his father tongue, and every two or three years he would visit his relatives in Offenburg, near the Alsatian border.

Surely the woman who had left the book behind was a German tourist. He decided she had to be a woman because of how she had placed the book. Facedown on the floor or head down on a shelf, it doesn't matter, he declared, it's a feminine trait. When he left the hotel he realized she was also an Ungaretti fan because on the facade was a commemorative plaque that read:

IN THIS BUILDING

DURING THE SUMMER OF 1913

LIVED

THE ITALIAN POET

GIUSEPPE UNGARETTI

1888–1970

The last date was also the year of his marriage. He had met Joyce the year before, in a place in La Mancha, he used to say, on the ferry between Dover and Calais. Among large black storm clouds, the high cliffs rose like white fairy castles.

He recited to her fragments of an epiphany of the young James Joyce on the ferry taking him home. *The sea moves with the sound of many scales* . . . The sea once again spattered with scales.

He let himself be carried away by memories, back to Notre Dame, to that summer night in 1969 when they kissed—for the first time—in front of the illuminated cathedral. (And when they lived in Buffalo, Joyce hung a reproduction of a 1902 painting by Matisse, *Notre-Dame en fin d'après-midi*, in the bedroom facing the bed, to remind them of their *vie en rose* in Paris.) Moments after he explained to Joyce in detail that on Good Friday 1903 the nonbeliever James Joyce attended the Tenebrae service at Notre Dame Cathedral and then wandered the streets for two hours reciting his own epiphanies and at eleven that night returned to his hotel, the Grand Hôtel Corneille, at the corner of rues Corneille and Vaugirard, near the place de l'Odéon, where he found the famous telegram from his father asking him to come home because his mother was dying. At midnight, as a last resort, he woke a champagne merchant whom he tutored, who lent him the seventy-five francs he needed to return to Dublin the next morning.

She began to notice the dampness of the night, and she leaned, *en douce,* against his shoulder.

Twenty-five years later he was looking again into the black river of remembrance, *Questa è la Senna* . . . and in its dark reflections he recognized himself flailing his arms in despair. Recently he'd been having too many dreams about deaths and accidents, and sometimes in the small hours his own shouts would wake him. Catharsis? The laughter and lightheartedness of youth had been left far behind.

Their next French kiss was on place Boucicaut, near the boulevard Raspail, though Reck spelled it Boucicault.

That was the night of his birthday, and it turned out that she had also turned thirty-two just one day before, on June 26. My senior, my seniorita.

They celebrated at an Alsatian restaurant near the Théâtre de l'Odéon, and the Rhine wine—das Rheingold, as Reck said—went to her head. Gleeful with glasses of Riesling, he told her that James Joyce had also preferred white wine, electricity, he called it, and Reck listed for her the writer's favorites: Swiss Fendant de Sion, French Clos Saint Patrice . . .

She was charmed by the red bodices and long black hair ribbons of the waitresses. She also liked the plates decorated with rustic Alsatian scenes. A few days later he gave her

*L'Ami Fritz* by Erckmann-Chatrian and a book of Hansi's illustrations and caricatures.

After much aimless wandering it is possible he returned to the Alsatian restaurant because it was June 27 again, but Reck only noted in French: *Un triste repas.* Or perhaps he wrote "repose." And after that, also in French: *Ennuis,* sorrows. Unless he wrote *Ennis.* Back at the hotel he recalled that after their supper watered with Rhine wine, Joyce and he had seen on the carrefour de l'Odéon, almost deserted at that hour, an old clocharde as thin and livid as a mummy who pissed standing up and when she was finished deftly wiped herself with a roll of pink toilet paper that she unfurled like a streamer. They laughingly hailed the mission completed, the micturation of l'eau de l'Odéon . . . Then, so as not to waver or stray from the principal current, he told his probably puritan compatriot that James Joyce's first masturbation, portrait of the onanist as a young man, occurred in the country after he heard the maid, who had taken him and his brothers out for a walk, peeing behind some bushes. Perhaps there was some "pipiphany" that marked the occasion. In Paris, by the way, James Joyce had a parrot named Pipi.

Reck returned to the hotel when it was past midnight, and after he rang for a very long time, a slatternly older woman with a woebegone face opened the door and immediately returned to the reception desk and resumed grumbling into the phone. He heard her repeat several times: *Salaud! Salaud! Tu es un vrai salaud, Pierre!*

Reck decided to use the stairs and avoid the oppressiveness of the narrow elevator, and in spite of this he dreamed that night he was traveling down a river, presumably the

Seine, lying in a black barge, and suddenly the funereal vessel became a coffin plunging over a waterfall that resembled the one in Saint-Cloud park. Later he recalled that on his first visit to Paris he had gone with Joyce to Saint-Cloud park, which James Joyce had also visited on his twenty-first birthday. And afterward they went to the theater. Oh *les beaux jours*.

The next morning he was nostalgic for the good times in the Luxembourg Garden, where his wife had loved to stroll. In front of the display window at the José Corti bookstore on the rue Médicis, he recalled that in 1931 a madman from Trieste named Corti had written death threats to James Joyce.

When he walked past the stalls of the *bouquinistes* along the Seine, he recalled that this was where Joyce had bought him the sepia postcard of the rooftops of Paris in a black frame, the legend at the bottom also written in sepia ink: *Paris pour Paradis* . . . They hadn't known if it was a line from some poem or simply a catchphrase, but they adopted it as the joyful motto of Paris and their paradise. There is no more par . . . , he wrote, perhaps an abbreviation. The view on the old postcard was probably taken from Notre Dame: on the left edge one could see the dark shape of a gargoyle, unless it was the hunchback . . . they sometimes joked.

Then he went to the rue Edmond-Valentin, between avenues Rapp and Bosquet, in the seventh arrondissement, where he and his wife had lived in a garret during a sabbatical in 1975. He called it his sub-attical year. When he passed number 7, he always looked up to the top floor, the fifth: James Joyce had lived there from February 1, 1935, to April 15, 1939. A bronze plaque beside the door recalls that Ricardo

Güiraldes, the Argentine writer, died in that house on October 8, 1927. Did they live on the same floor? Though Valéry Larbaud was a friend and advocate of both, in all probability Joyce had never heard of Güiraldes or *Don Segundo Sombra*. He would have liked the shadow-filled title.

Reck continued then along the avenue Bosquet and turned left onto the rue de Grenelle until he reached the place Robiac, also in the seventh, where Joyce had lived earlier, beginning in 1925. His sweetest home, he wrote, there on the third floor. Reck recalled that in the interval between two heavy downpours he had photographed Joyce sitting on a bench in front of the house, on her lap a children's book by the Countess of Ségur, *Après la pluie le beau temps,* which she pretended to be reading diligently, marking each line with her index finger. With bibliomaniacal precision Reck may have noted the page and line she pointed to: Ségur 95-20.

He retraced his steps along the avenue Bosquet to the pont de l'Alma and said to himself in writing: How often Joyce and I contemplated the tawny Seine from this bridge. And gauged the height of the water around the gigantic Zouave of that support column. Now it doesn't even reach the soles of his boots. When she looked at it, did Joyce ever think of the expression *faire le zouave,* to play the clown?

He ate in the brasserie on the place de l'Alma where Joyce and he particularly enjoyed the oysters. Chez Francis. In the days of hefty grants. He saw her come in impetuously, shaking her coppery curls and an indomitable umbrella. *Après le parapluie, le déluge* . . . he would joke when she reached the table. Where are the rains of yesteryear? *Europe après la pluie,* by Max Ernst, was the only contemporary painting that ever interested Joyce, which may have been why Reck passed on that interest to his wife, who at the time was preparing a study of the Franco-German painter. The importance of being Ernst.

In an essay that Joyce dedicated to Mons, in the American magazine *ArtNews,* she also refers to Ernst's photomontage techniques in connection with Mons's "Monstrages" and his work as an illustrator—or *illuminator,* as she calls it—of the *Epiphanies.*

A couple came in, two plump, pompous bourgeois who inevitably made him think of certain caricatures by Grosz, the other contemporary painter whom Joyce viewed with unclouded eyes. An excruciatingly thin lady, wearing a hat and coat despite the heat, considered him between sips of consommé. He looked away, at the matron with the V-shaped décolletage that displayed her opulent nanny-goat udders. Just how Leopold Bloom and his creator liked them.

He returned to the hotel for a short siesta because of the almost Sevillean heat; perhaps he was exaggerating. After taking a shower, with many a slip, he went out to visit the bookstores on and around the rue des Écoles. After that he drank beer and made notes on the terrace of L'Écritoire, on the place de la Sorbonne. Next to him someone raised *Le Monde* like a wall. Out of the corner of his eye he read the headlines.

RWANDA: L ÉNIGME DE LA BÊTE NOIRE

He realized his error; context can so easily deceive. Instead of *bête noire,* of course, it said *boîte noire.* It would make a good title for a novel: *The Enigma of the Black Box.* By Maurice Leblanc.

BOSNIE-HERZÉGOVINE, in another headline, made him see the transubstantiation of wine into blood and not the golden liquid of the archduchess that Joyce liked so much.

He continued his excursion through memory along the rue Racine, the place Saint-Sulpice . . . to the intersection of Sèvres-Babylone, a combination his wife adored, and he had to muster all his courage—he confessed—to go into the bar of the Hôtel Lutétia. (She liked its art deco decor, especially the sconces. And at the Lutétia bar I introduced her to Victor Mons, whose work she would promote in the United States. She always signed her writing with her maiden name, Joyce Adam, which her husband must have particularly enjoyed because more than once I heard him introduce her as his "Adam's rib.") I drink to remember, Reck wrote, and he saw her again in the shadows, sitting beside him and sneaking an occasional sip of his Bloody Molly, as she called it. For a brief impulsive moment he thought about staying at the Lutétia this time, too. The hotel where he and Joyce had spent their first night in Paris on their *pleine lune de miel,* he wrote in French. The same hotel where Joyce spent his last two months in Paris, from October 15 to December 23, 1939, he wrote with precision, before undertaking his final journey into exile and silence. At the reception desk in the Lutétia they had known nothing about Mr. Joyce or which room might have been his, but when they saw the couple so disappointed they suggested room 711, where General de Gaulle had spent his wedding night. They did not aim so high, but in another room two floors down they achieved their objective, their goal. *Mon Général* . . . she called him, not yet knowing that during the Occupation the Lutétia had been the headquarters of the German counterespionage agency. Later, on the balcony, they had kissed again across from place Boucicaut. And again Reck added an L to the square. And wrote that only in his imagination did he dare go up to their old room. When he opened the door, Joyce's silhouette was outlined against the chiaroscuro of the balcony. The dead don't come back, he observed bitterly, and he decided to go out into the present night.

He ate very little at the Closerie des Lilas, only bisque and Rhine wine. *Power house,* more electrical fluid, he noted. And recalled how he and Joyce had laughed as they repeated, in French and in English, Young man, I say unto thee, Arise . . . after he told her that in this very restaurant James Joyce had spoken to a young Irishman named Power about the power of words, particularly English words, and tried to convince him of the superiority of English over French by resorting to biblical citations in the two languages. *Jeune homme, je te le dis, lève-toi,* Joyce pronounced the words badly in her Yankee accent, perhaps in too loud a voice, and the waiter thought they were arguing.

Reck continued to relive other times and consume more drinks in Montparnasse. Since the death of his wife he had resumed drinking too much. And smoking. He had also abandoned the dictatorial regime Joyce had imposed on him in recent years to control his diabetes.

On his way back to the hotel, at the corner of the rue des Carmes and place Maubert, he was tempted by the lively terrace of the Village Ronsard, and he went in for a nightcap.

Leaning on the bar, a big-bellied boozer about his age, wearing shorts and sandals with socks, maintained that a man isn't old as long as he doesn't think he's old. Will I be old soon? Joyce, at his age, was already in the next world. I feel old without Joyce, he concluded.

He recognized the dark-haired girl writing postcards at the next table. He had seen her that morning in the hotel dining room, wearing the same dress with red roses, cut very low in the back, where he could count all her bones. She'd had breakfast alone, and he saw in her an air of bewilderment, perhaps because of her staring dark eyes, which reminded him of Sylvia Beach, the owner of the bookstore Shakespeare and Company, on the rue de l'Odéon, and the first publisher of *Ulysses. Les roses étaient toutes rouges,* Reck recited the *vers* by Verlaine. A red rose on the dress of his daughter-in-law was the first thing James Joyce saw after his tenth or perhaps eleventh cataract operation in 1930. A red rose is a rose . . . though Miss Stein was not his favorite Gertrude.

She also recognized the solitary guest in the Ronsard before he said a word to her. They began speaking in French but soon changed to German because she was Swiss, from Basel.

What immediately caught her eye on his table was the notebook with the portrait of James Joyce on its cover, though she didn't know who the elegantly dressed gentleman was; he reminded her of a magician who performed in a hotel-resort in Baden-Baden under the name of Mephisto.

(*Le carnet du Diable,* Reck wrote in parentheses, no doubt recalling the title of the operetta James Joyce had seen in Rome one Sunday early in February 1907, in the company of Nora—already pregnant with Lucia—and their two-year-old son, Giorgio. And perhaps he also remembered that some eleven years later, in Zurich, Giorgio's classmates claimed that his father resembled the Devil, and even the house-keeper they had at the time called him "Herr Satan.")

They talked about the Devil and Hell, in which she believed because she was a Catholic, though not a practicing one. She also believed that the souls of the dead sometimes communicate with the living, and she said that an aunt of hers in Basel was a medium. And in passing she added that at times she herself would suddenly write—without knowing why and wherever she might be—sentences that just slipped out as if someone were directing her hand. Occasionally even numbers that might have been formulas and equations, but they were Greek to her, which is what had happened one night last winter in the Hôtel Métropole in Brussels. She had worked as a chambermaid in good hotels in Switzerland, Belgium, and Germany. Most recently in France, and she mentioned the Hôtel Maison Rouge in Strasbourg and the Hôtel Suisse in Nice.

She turned her wide-open eyes again to the notebook with the portrait of Joyce and wrote rapidly—with a black ballpoint pen that said HÔTEL MÉTROPOLE in gilded letters, Reck recounted in detail—on the empty cigarette pack left in the ashtray on the table, a box of Players with the head of a bearded sailor in the center of a life preserver, and then handed it to Reck.

The first thing he read, scribbled inside the box in capital letters:

I WANT TO BE FRANK

He could not hide his confusion. How had she guessed his name?

But doubts and interpretations surfaced immediately. Did

it really say, in English, I want to be Frank, or I want to be sincere?

And then, in a more difficult hand, also in capitals, manifestly incongruous in antiquated French, the celebrated motto of the Abbey of Telema, Do what you will: FAY CE QUE VOULDRAS.

But, she assured him, she had never read François Rabelais. Frank, the anglicized diminutive of François for the frankest of authors. Joyce was frequently compared to Rabelais, by Valéry Larbaud and Edmond Jaloux, among others, Reck recalled. And who knows if a cat named François that Joyce had owned in Paris wasn't an implicit acknowledgment and allusion, since he never recognized his debt to Master François and even claimed he had never read him.

And under the French motto, a single English word: *Abbey*. And also in English, under that, as if in a poem, perhaps praise or publicity for the cigarette brand: *Excellent Players*. And on the next line, again in English, *Frantic sex,* or perhaps ambiguously *Frantic sack,* a furious pillage, or perhaps a paper bag or getting fired or a bed or even the white wine imported from Spain in the sixteenth and seventeenth centuries. Quarrelsome wine? Reck favored "furious pillage" because the next line said in French, "Your money or your life." The chambermaid must have been used to the garbled gabble or Babelic potpourri of international hotels because Reck thought he could make out *Dime,* tell me, in Spanish, unless it was the American ten-cent coin. And then with repeated urgency: *Presto presto,* in Italian, or maybe it was Spanish again, I lend I lend, another ambiguity.

She continued to stare at him with wide-open eyes, and Reck, as if hypnotized, handed her Joyce's notebook, open, its pages blank. She filled three pages with a flying ballpoint pen, blue filaments like veins, a strange stenography (or "sternography," perhaps, because those mysterious pages reminded him of certain passages with filiform scrawls in *Tristram Shandy*) in which Reck recognized with concealed emotion occasional words in various languages. Fearful fabulations? He realized that the poor chambermaid did not understand her own automatic writing, and he could scarcely contain his impatience—Joyce's notebook and the Players package were burning in his hand—as he hurriedly paid both their checks so he could retire to the hotel and calmly begin the work of deciphering.

When they were walking up the rue des Carmes toward the hotel, he told her in a strangled voice that she had clairvoyantly guessed his name. Had she really? She said her name was Augusta, and he, immune by this time to astonishment, acknowledged that destiny masterfully plays with symmetries because in a crematorium in Augusta, the capital of Maine, where Joyce had come from originally, the body of his wife had flown as smoke up to the sky along with the manuscript of the epiphanies that he had placed in the casket next to her as a funerary offering. It was also his Christmas present.

Reck spent most of the night trying to decipher the fly and ant or palinsect tracks in Joyce's notebook. At times it reminded him of the automatic writing of George, Yeats's wife. Though James Joyce admired Yeats's poetry, in particular "A Vision," and in his youth had read books on the occult, he remained skeptical regarding manifestations of the beyond. "The only spirit I believe in is *l'esprit de l'escalier*," he joked at the dinner party for his forty-sixth birthday in

Paris, when his friend the bookstore owner Adrienne Monnier began to talk about rotating tables and the messages she and some friends had received from certain spirits.

And yet, and Yeats . . . And still . . . Reck recalled that Joyce had confessed to his closest friend in Zurich, the painter Frank Budgen, that he believed the theory of certain occultists that essential ideas are, like matter, indestructible, and are stored in some receptacle situated outside space and time to which the mind has access at certain privileged moments. At times Joyce's vision coincided with that of Yeats. But Joyce was more concerned with oculists than occultists, Reck concedes, and with reason. *Borsch and Tears,* he added, alluding with a touch of lachrymal humor both to Dr. Borsch, a Parisian ophthalmologist who performed several operations on Joyce, and to a popular pseudo-Russian restaurant in London.

Joyce also had blind faith in the clairvoyant power of his mad daughter. Lucia the Second-Sighted . . .

Abruptly he reexamined the Players pack, prey to persistent doubts.

*Frantic sack,* that furious pillaging in the play between money and life—wasn't it an allusion to František Schaurek, James Joyce's Czech brother-in-law, married to his sister Eileen, whom he affectionately called Frank? Schaurek worked at a bank in Trieste and committed suicide in 1926, blowing his brains out when he could not return the money (some seventy-five thousand francs) he had embezzled from the bank. And then, rereading carefully, Reck thought the English word *Abbey* might well have been *At bay.* And didn't it say *Excellent Payers* instead of *Players*? The bank had given him a month to return the money. But at the time neither

James Joyce nor his brother Stanislaus could help him financially, though Eileen had sent a telegram to James announcing that František was ruined, *Frank rovinato*, and asking him to save them. His life not worth a cent? And do what you will a cynical invitation to suicide? On occasion Joyce had been angry with his brother-in-law, for example at a birthday party in Trieste.

Reck was lost in a sea of doubts, in the ebb and flow of a vast ocean, because the Irishman's entire work is awash in doubt. Even Joyce acknowledges, in one of his rare effusive moments, that life is suspended in doubt like the world in empty space.

Was Schaurek really that Frank?

Then he connected Fay and *Abbey*. Frank Fay! he wrote with an exclamation point, one of two brothers who were actors, first in the National Theatre Society and then at the Abbey Theatre in Dublin, yes, the players at the Abbey whom Joyce called "excellent actors" in a limerick, following a bout of serious drinking that he slept off in one of the passageways in the theater while they were rehearsing, which would explain "Excellent Players." Players? He had his doubts again. In Zurich, during the First World War, Joyce founded a theater company, The English Players, or simply Players for short, whose manager was also named Frank, Frank Gschwind, and Reck must have suffered a veritable vertigo of revelatory writing because in his hurried handwriting he wrote, incorrectly, *Geschwindel*, vertiginous velocity.

*Presto presto*, with *dimes* and *diretes*, tell mes and I'll tell yous, and he recalled the *"Dimmi tutto, e presto presto"* in the beautiful Italian version of the Anna Livia Plurabelle episode translated by James Joyce in collaboration with his *caro signor* Frank, Nino Frank.

Neither no nor yes, a sinuous coming and going of insidious insinuations, until Reck suddenly recognized him, saw the (sad?) face of the red-bearded sailor in the central circle of the labyrinth-pack of Players, and he must have shouted FRANK! before writing it down in capital letters, Frank, the sailor renounced at the last moment by a frightened Eveline in the title story of *Dubliners*, who stayed behind in port, disconsolate and without a sweetheart, perhaps heading for spinsterhood in some abbey where she will never wear white and on top of that will have to be the sole support of her drunken father. And frantic sex would be left for the sailor who would have love, a new love taken and a new leave-taking in every port. Perhaps James Joyce secretly wanted to be that freewheeling sailor in free port after free port: didn't he sometimes call himself the Ancient Mariner, and after *Finnegans Wake* didn't he plan to write a plain and simple book on the perpetually self-perpetuating sea?

Reck felt that he had lost his footing, that he was submerged again in a black sea of signs and doubts—and erroneous meditations?

It was hot, and he opened the window wide: bursts of a sports broadcast and screaming fans reached him. Bra-zil, Bra-zil . . . *It's not cricket,* and he also noted that cricket was the only sport that had really interested James Joyce. He went to bed too late, still conjecturing, and spent his few hours of sleep, or rather nightmare, tossed by tempests, torments, and deaths. Reck was also terrified of electrical storms and told himself he would ask Augusta if she knew of a hotel in Basel called Three Kings. Or better yet, cringes, because in that hotel, one stormy afternoon in August 1937, during a lightning-streaked tea, Joyce suddenly leaped up and left his guests to cower in his room, under the bed, perhaps, or in a closet.

Reck went down to the dining room after nine in the morning and did not see Augusta. After breakfast he inquired at the reception desk and was informed—though she hadn't registered and they didn't know her first or last name—that the mademoiselle in Room 34 had left for good an hour ago.

It is easy to imagine his distress: he had lost her. He probably supposed she was the inexhaustible mine—or pencil, perhaps—that would reveal to him the hidden veins, the poetic veins in the epiphanies that were lost or perhaps only imagined and never written, the true epiphanies without end.

An empty pack of cigarettes and three pages of almost indecipherable automatic scribbling were mere samples— free samples?—of a treasure that had vanished with the chambermaid who would never even suspect she had been amanuensis to Joyce.

It is no easy task to follow all the steps—most of them false—taken by Reck in Paris on that nearly ashen Wednesday. In Aux Deux Magots he wrote to several colleagues and friends. To Jacques Aubert, in Lyon, saying he had missed him in Seville and was going to buy a new copy of his Pléiade Joyce. To Loni and David Hayman, explaining that this time he probably couldn't visit them at their summerhouse in Maine. To Mons he sent a clipping that reproduced his portrait of Joyce. She had liked his painting her dressed so charmingly in a beret and dotted dress . . . he assured him. He wrote to Mons at his farm-studio in Enfer (and singularized the address: chemin d'Averne, with no final S), though he wondered where Mons could be wandering. And he told me he was in Paris, that unexpected and sensational discoveries were changing his vision of the epiphanies, and he hoped to call me soon.

He had the notebook with the hieroglyphs that he attempted to decipher in various cafés in the Latin Quarter, perhaps in the secret hope that he would run into Augusta. Was his search absurd? Elusive or illusive?

At the Cluny he was disheartened as he contemplated again the clown in the beret on the tie in the portrait of James Joyce.

In reality the author of *Ulysses* thought this 1934 portrait by Jacques-Émile Blanche was awful, and the only thing that pleased his almost blind eyes was the tie. James Joyce and the esthetic of the tie, a study still to be written. In his period as a Paris dandy, beginning in the 1920s, when he wrote or wove his Penelopean winding sheet subsidized by his patron Miss Weaver, he managed to amass a rich collection of ties. And when he posed in Paris in 1924 for the young Irish painter Patrick Tuohy, who spoke to him of how important it was for an artist to capture the soul of his subject, Joyce cut him off by requesting that he just get his tie right.

He opened the notebook and in the tangle of lines he translated or deciphered, at the Cluny:

Clown. My crown for 1 livre. 10 francs. Tours de passe-passe-partout. Clown & clown. Almost Siamese twins, insep-arable, on that trip. Nous n'irons plus au Bois.

No doubt Reck misread Clown, it should have been

because in that hotel, one stormy afternoon in August 1937, during a lightning-streaked tea, Joyce suddenly leaped up and left his guests to cower in his room, under the bed, perhaps, or in a closet.

Reck went down to the dining room after nine in the morning and did not see Augusta. After breakfast he inquired at the reception desk and was informed—though she hadn't registered and they didn't know her first or last name—that the mademoiselle in Room 34 had left for good an hour ago.

It is easy to imagine his distress: he had lost her. He probably supposed she was the inexhaustible mine—or pencil, perhaps—that would reveal to him the hidden veins, the poetic veins in the epiphanies that were lost or perhaps only imagined and never written, the true epiphanies without end.

An empty pack of cigarettes and three pages of almost indecipherable automatic scribbling were mere samples—free samples?—of a treasure that had vanished with the chambermaid who would never even suspect she had been amanuensis to Joyce.

It is no easy task to follow all the steps—most of them false—taken by Reck in Paris on that nearly ashen Wednesday.

In Aux Deux Magots he wrote to several colleagues and friends. To Jacques Aubert, in Lyon, saying he had missed him in Seville and was going to buy a new copy of his Pléiade Joyce. To Loni and David Hayman, explaining that this time he probably couldn't visit them at their summerhouse in Maine. To Mons he sent a clipping that reproduced his portrait of Joyce. She had liked his painting her dressed so charmingly in a beret and dotted dress . . . he assured him. He wrote to Mons at his farm-studio in Enfer (and singularized the address: chemin d'Averne, with no final S), though he wondered where Mons could be wandering. And he told me he was in Paris, that unexpected and sensational discoveries were changing his vision of the epiphanies, and he hoped to call me soon.

He had the notebook with the hieroglyphs that he attempted to decipher in various cafés in the Latin Quarter, perhaps in the secret hope that he would run into Augusta. Was his search absurd? Elusive or illusive?

At the Cluny he was disheartened as he contemplated again the clown in the beret on the tie in the portrait of James Joyce.

In reality the author of *Ulysses* thought this 1934 portrait by Jacques-Émile Blanche was awful, and the only thing that pleased his almost blind eyes was the tie. James Joyce and the esthetic of the tie, a study still to be written. In his period as a Paris dandy, beginning in the 1920s, when he wrote or wove his Penelopean winding sheet subsidized by his patron Miss Weaver, he managed to amass a rich collection of ties. And when he posed in Paris in 1924 for the young Irish painter Patrick Tuohy, who spoke to him of how important it was for an artist to capture the soul of his subject, Joyce cut him off by requesting that he just get his tie right.

He opened the notebook and in the tangle of lines he translated or deciphered, at the Cluny:

Clown. My crown for 1 livre. 10 francs. Tours de passe-passe-partout. Clown & clown. Almost Siamese twins, insep-arable, on that trip. Nous n'irons plus au Bois.

No doubt Reck misread Clown, it should have been

Chown, a Siamese student whom Joyce met at the Biblio-
thèque Sainte-Geneviève in Paris in 1903, and with whom he
made an excursion to Tours—with the ten francs he lent
him—that would prove very profitable because at the kiosk
in the station at Tours he bought a copy of *Les Lauriers sont
coupés,* by Édouard Dujardin, which unlocked for him the
gate or floodgates of interior monologue. There is no evi-
dence, however, that Joyce ever made an excursion to the
Bois de Boulogne with Chown.

The next passage, as multilingual as it is equivocal, may
possibly have been deciphered by Reck at the same café:

La Maison des Amis. I want to be frank. [The same old
song!] Der Mensch ist Gut. It isn't good for a good man to
be alone. The old patriarch staggering at the door, drunk
between the two *filles* with feather boas who tug at his beard.
Oui, mes poules. Noé d'Odéon.

Professor Reck wondered if this scene was really situated
on the rue de l'Odéon, perhaps at the door to Adrienne
Monnier's bookstore La Maison des Amis des Livres, or at
the Café Odéon in Zurich, which Joyce had frequented.

Paris was a palimpsest of evocations, above all of Joyce in
connection with Joyce, a labyrinth no less intricate than the
one in the notebook he was struggling to get through. Sitting on a tier of the amphitheater of Lutèce, behind the rue
Monge, he thought he was correctly following some errant
words:

Shifting stones and pieces. Pebbles. Oberisks—. In the
bottomless unfunded laborinth. Bottoms up! Cul sec de sac!
Salud! Tunnel to the end of the tun. Weave threads of fire-
flies. Turkic tippler weaves an inflamed rainbow. Weber &

Weaver. Sad schemer weaving tangled plots. Sob . . . sober. Oberond or drunken ass? India inkblottery. Night at the end of the tunnel. Lucicécité.

Reck interprets this passage as a reminiscence of the game called "Le Labyrinthe," which Joyce bought in Franz Karl Weber's shop on Bahnhofstrasse in Zurich and played at night with his daughter Lucia at the time he was preparing the chapter "Wandering Rocks" in *Ulysses*. He associates the names of the merchant Weber and of his future benefactor Miss Weaver (both names have the same meaning) with Bottom the Weaver in *A Midsummer Night's Dream*. Miss Weaver, a Quaker, was permanently preoccupied by Joyce's alcohol—and ocular—problems. And he, in a letter dated November 9, 1927, tells her he had a dream in which a Turk was weaving in a bazaar with tangled skeins the colors of the rainbow.

It is possible that on this Wednesday Reck visited the cemetery of Père-Lachaise, because he noted in a Franglais of dubious taste:

Whoever went to Seville perd la chaise? Engraved gravestones. Cryptes à décrypter . . . Père Goriot, where?

In any case his transcriptions grow somber, become even more confused, among tombs and tombstones.

Black slab elaborately chiseled, he transcribes. Moi seul aussi, Frau Meissel. Mournful mausoleum. I too am a frightened stag. (A clear allusion to the wife of Filippo Meissel, Ada Hirsch Meissel, who committed suicide. Joyce and he visited her grave in the Trieste cemetery one day in the fall of 1912.)

Suicides in life and literature intermingle in the confused lines of the notebook:

Incurable acolyte without a curate for his own funeral mass. Ite messia est . . . Anointed of the Lord. The first. Ur-Bloom. Bloom úr. Zombie of Szombathely. Ur-ur-gent. Silhouettes, lethal. Monk's cowl? Astounded. Drain the cup . . . To your hemlock! Take away this cup if you can . . . Monkshood. Yellow grimace.

Recollection of Leopold Bloom's father, of Hungarian origin, who changed his name from Virag to Bloom and committed suicide with monkshood in the Queen's Hotel of Ennis on June 27, 1886. (Yesterday was our anniversary, Reck recalled.)

Don't raise the lid? A suicide who blew off the top of his head. And then he transcribes in German "A horrible sight!" *Schaurig!* or more likely *Schaurek!* the name of Joyce's Czech brother-in-law.

Reck suspects that his suicide must have made an especially deep impression on Joyce (Schaurek lay unconscious for twenty-six hours after the fatal shot) and must also have left him with an especially bad conscience because he could not help his sister Eileen when she sent him an SOS from Dublin (*Salveci!*, save us) and did not even have the courage to tell her that Schaurek had committed suicide when she passed through Paris on her way back to Trieste. As on other occasions, this unpleasant role fell to the other brother, Stanislaus. Eileen refused to accept her husband's death and ordered the coffin opened.

Reck continued going round and round the seventh circle because then he transcribed an allusion to the painter Patrick Tuohy, who committed suicide in New York in 1930:

*C'è calco di tuo in quella brutta faccia. New Work in New York. Specktrickular mask. Death is also a funky facepainter.* (That pale face is your spitting image.) Joyce called Tuohy *Funny face-painter* in a limerick he wrote in 1927. There is also a possible allusion to Paul Speck, the sculptor from Zurich who made James Joyce's death mask.

Then Reck becomes Dantesque and transcribes: We who were men are now no more than weeds. Talking shrubs. Husky-voiced trunks. Parroting laurels. Pierres des vignes sauvages. Perhaps an allusion to the poet-suicide Pierre des Vignes, who appears in Canto XIII of the *Inferno*. In 1933, a certain Dr. Vignes treated Lucia Joyce for her mental agitation and to honor his name recommended she drink wine with meals. And he grapples with the paradox—an entwining vine—for anyone so fond of the grape that Joyce lived on the rue des Vignes from April to August 1939. It was, in fact, his last Parisian residence.

The allusions become entangled in that forest of suicides, in trench warfare that refers to Trench, the model for Haines in *Ulysses*, who had nightmares about panthers that he frightened away by shooting at them and who also committed suicide by shooting himself in the head. And then, death by water in the Thames, the tomb of Cosgrave, who receives the name of Lynch in *Ulysses;* but in spite of Stephen's prophecy, *Et laqueo se suspendit*, he died not by hanging but by drowning, in 1926, perhaps after drowning his sorrows in alcohol.

The black sun of melancholy, *caresse triste*, next to a cross, was a memento or monument to the editor of The Black Sun Press, Harry Crosby, who published a fragment of *Finnegans Wake* and committed suicide in New York on December 10, 1929. Not long afterward Joyce sent a condolence telegram to his wife, Caresse.

In that cemetery in Joyce's notebook there appeared *un Angelo sfortunato* muffled in his own wings as if they were a cape, who was another editor, the Italian Angelo Fortunato Formiggini, to whom Joyce suggested without success the publication in a single volume of his nine articles in Italian that had appeared in the *Piccolo della Sera* of Trieste. Formiggini, a socialist and a Jew, committed suicide in 1938 when the race laws were introduced in Italy.

Reck normally smoked American cigarettes from his birthplace, Virginia, but influenced perhaps by his obsession he bought a pack of Players, English Players—he underlined the phrase—in a bar-tabac on the rue du Cardinal Lemoine (recalling the repugnance his wife had felt for tobacco, he noted: Joyce would not say this smoke smells of roses) and smoking as he sat on the terrace, he continued his deciphering:

Neither no nor yes. In the center of the bifurcaution [*sic*]. Or perhaps he wrote *"bifurcanzone."* Because on the next line he noted in French: Spring or summer, I am not the man they think. Reck believes this is an obvious allusion to Nino Frank, who arranged for Joyce to be on the editorial board of the French magazine *Bifur*. Nino Frank also gave him a record of songs from the operetta *Trois valses,* on which Yvonne Printemps sang *Je ne suis pas ce que l'on pense,* a song that aroused Joyce's appreciation and apprehension.

In reality Reck may have been formulating a test project, reading his own recollections and obsessions into doubtful words of more than doubtful interpretation. Or perhaps he was attempting to re-create his *Epiphanies Without End* by other means. *Epis fanés,* his own crop, an Augustan harvest. Reck refers, funereal thoughts once more, to the mummification of the moment. To fix the ephemeral, he writes in French and signs it with his own initials: F.M.R.

He reconstructed yet another ephemerid:

Canaan's can. Kanne blanche. Noces de canaille. They've forgotten the wine! Noise de Sion . . . Strident shrieks of peacocks. Another round. Another accident. Change of direction, again. Wiederkehr. Another turn. Dangerous devolution of divine wine. From life to death. Sadly I remade it. All via crucis lead to Zurich. Another change of direction. The Prince de gale, of Wails, in his sports car. Borach und Krach! Fatal crash. Funeral car. Alfa Romeo and Omega.

A passage referring to an old student and dear friend of Joyce's from Zurich, Georges Borach, who killed himself driving a sports car on March 13, a Good Friday, in 1934. A few days later Joyce passed by the scene of the accident in a car on a trip from Monte Carlo to Zurich. There is also a reference to the Pfauen Café in Zurich, which Borach frequented in the company of Joyce, and to Fendant de Sion, the house wine, supplied by another old student and friend of Joyce's, Paul Wiederkehr.

The final transcription, he insists:

Le 13 revient. Deus ex macchina. Partire è un po' morire. Guarda in Treviso la morte. Le ossa rotte, Ettore. Senza perder l'autocoscienza. Una vita non vale una cicca. R.I.P. Ultima sigla retta.

(The 13th returns. Fate in an automobile. Parting is dying a little. Look death in the face in Treviso. Broken bones, Ettore. Without losing autoconsciousness. A life isn't worth anything. R.I.P. The final literal abbreviation.)

Ettore Schmidt, alias Italo Svevo, the author of *La co-*

*scienza di Zeno,* a student and friend of Joyce's in Trieste, had an automobile accident near Treviso on September 13, 1928, and died shortly afterward.

As he passed the restaurant Balzar, on the rue des Écoles, Reck thought of Balzac and noted *Fuge . . . Late . . . Tace,* the motto that Joyce had taken from *Le Médecin de campagne* and translated as silence, exile, and cunning. Reck wondered if he should look for that novel before eating. Balzar or Balzac? He'll eat first, he decides. *Primum vivere.* Cross to the other side afterward. Joyce, et Compagnie . . . may possibly refer to the Compagnie bookstore on the other side of the street.

(The school of Joyce faces the school of Proust, he noted later in parentheses, a probable reference to the École Berlitz, over the Compagnie bookstore and almost directly across from the cours Marcel Proust in the building next to the restaurant Balzar.)

He ordered a liver steak and a Burgundy, a red Meursault that Joyce in disgust had called liquid steak but that Leopold Bloom savored with pleasure. One more swallow, and he added in French, *pour que tout soit consommé.*

Drinking more than usual, he confirms, a sad clinical decline. Or is it cynical?

And he smoked one cigarette after the other and never stopped thinking that his wife would find the sweetish aroma repugnant. It isn't exactly the smoke of roses, she would tell him, and he would unfailingly recall that James Joyce had once smoked a cigarette made of rose petals offered him by an adolescent girl who was one of his students in Trieste. Hidden emanations. In fact, his wife once reproached him during an argument, one summer in the house of Reck's parents in Virginia, near the Chesapeake Bay, that he had told her many more details about the life of James Joyce than about his own.

Reck brought the pack of Players close to his eyes and thought he could decipher, in white letters, on the blue cap of the sailor: NEMO. So then he was, in some way, Ulysses, Joyce's favorite hero. Or did it say HERO? A good many doubts for so few letters. Much Ado About Nothing . . . He examined the pack again and copied down, perhaps with nostalgia, FINEST VIRGINIA. But he also noted immediately afterward extremely dangerous to your health, NUIT GRAVE-MENT A LA SAINTE, he made a mistake, he wrote "saintly woman" instead of "health," SANTÉ. Joyce, his wife, would have laughed and agreed.

Greenish blue sea behind the bust of the sailor.

He recalled in writing that as a boy he would run along the beach at dusk imitating the cries of the gulls.

FINEST VIRGINIA. U.S.

The last thing he wrote in Joyce's notebook.

At about two in the afternoon witnesses saw him at the door of the restaurant looking to the right and left, over and over again, as if searching for someone or perhaps trying to avoid someone, before he began to cross the rue des Écoles at a very rapid pace though he could not avoid the taxi bearing down on him.

He regained consciousness after a few hours, in the Hôpital Cochin, and the prognosis seemed hopeful until four days later when he fell unexpectedly into a deep coma from which he never awoke. When I visited him two days after the accident, he was extremely depressed and seemed distracted, but he smiled ironically when I reminded him that *scienza di Zeno,* a student and friend of Joyce's in Trieste, had an automobile accident near Treviso on September 13, 1928, and died shortly afterward.

As he passed the restaurant Balzar, on the rue des Écoles, Reck thought of Balzac and noted *Fuge . . . Late . . . Tace,* the motto that Joyce had taken from *Le Médecin de campagne* and translated as silence, exile, and cunning. Reck wondered if he should look for that novel before eating. Balzar or Balzac? He'll eat first, he decides. *Primum vivere.* Cross to the other side afterward. Joyce, et Compagnie . . . may possibly refer to the Compagnie bookstore on the other side of the street.

(The school of Joyce faces the school of Proust, he noted later in parentheses, a probable reference to the École Berlitz, over the Compagnie bookstore and almost directly across from the cours Marcel Proust in the building next to the restaurant Balzar.)

He ordered a liver steak and a Burgundy, a red Meursault that Joyce in disgust had called liquid steak but that Leopold Bloom savored with pleasure. One more swallow, and he added in French, *pour que tout soit consommé.*

Drinking more than usual, he confirms, a sad clinical decline. Or is it cynical?

And he smoked one cigarette after the other and never stopped thinking that his wife would find the sweetish aroma repugnant. It isn't exactly the smoke of roses, she would tell him, and he would unfailingly recall that James Joyce had once smoked a cigarette made of rose petals offered him by an adolescent girl who was one of his students in Trieste. Hidden emanations. In fact, his wife once reproached him during an argument, one summer in the house of Reck's parents in Virginia, near the Chesapeake Bay, that he had told her many more details about the life of James Joyce than about his own.

Reck brought the pack of Players close to his eyes and thought he could decipher, in white letters, on the blue cap of the sailor: NEMO. So then he was, in some way, Ulysses, Joyce's favorite hero. Or did it say HERO? A good many doubts for so few letters. Much Ado About Nothing . . . He examined the pack again and copied down, perhaps with nostalgia, FINEST VIRGINIA. But he also noted immediately afterward extremely dangerous to your health, NUIT GRAVE-MENT A LA SAINTE, he made a mistake, he wrote "saintly woman" instead of "health," SANTÉ. Joyce, his wife, would have laughed and agreed.

Greenish blue sea behind the bust of the sailor.

He recalled in writing that as a boy he would run along the beach at dusk imitating the cries of the gulls.

FINEST VIRGINIA. U.S.

The last thing he wrote in Joyce's notebook.

At about two in the afternoon witnesses saw him at the door of the restaurant looking to the right and left, over and over again, as if searching for someone or perhaps trying to avoid someone, before he began to cross the rue des Écoles at a very rapid pace though he could not avoid the taxi bearing down on him.

He regained consciousness after a few hours, in the Hôpital Cochin, and the prognosis seemed hopeful until four days later when he fell unexpectedly into a deep coma from which he never awoke. When I visited him two days after the accident, he was extremely depressed and seemed distracted, but he smiled ironically when I reminded him that he was in the same hospital where James Joyce had visited Samuel Beckett, who had been stabbed by a clochard, in January 1938.

I still ask myself why, in an envelope with my name written on it, which he dictated to a nurse, he left me Joyce's notebook. Perhaps because we spoke of his *Epiphanies Without End* in Dublin, Monte Carlo, and Seville. Or because he supposed I would sift through it and try to decipher it.

P.S. March 18, 1995. This morning when I passed by the hotel on the rue des Carmes, I particularly recalled Reck when I read the sign on the door:

Hôtel Fermé pour TRAVAUX
RÉNOVATIONS

Renovate or die?

I sat in the Ronsard, across from the Saturday market stalls on the place Maubert, and riffled through my tired hypotheses again. Accident, suicide? Reckless, rash? Did Reck really not know that almost on the same spot, and almost at the same hour, a little more than fourteen years earlier, the French critic Roland Barthes had been run down by a truck? Who had really written or dictated those seismographic pages that unleashed Reck's interpretations or deliriums? Perhaps they are contagious, because with each new reading new hypotheses emerge. A notebook of multiplying accounts and accounts that multiply.

P.P.S. August 30, 1997. Speaking at Chez Francis with Mons and the Swiss art editor and fervent Joycean, Max

Herz, about the possibility of a bibliophile's edition of Joyce's notebook, with the title *Paris pour Paradis,* Herz commented on his astonishment that Professor Reck had not realized that the painter Frank Budgen, James Joyce's friend in Zurich, had been the model for the sailor represented on the Players cigarette pack. Herz also believes that the final letters in Joyce's notebook, the u.s. after FINEST VIRGINIA, did not mean the United States but alluded to the *ultima sigaretta* in *La coscienza di Zeno* and to its author's last cigarette. Ultimate Svevo . . . Hypotheses that open new doubts and hypotheses. No doubt they won't be the last.

# Bullfight in Berlin

# I

ADALBERT STOCK copied or completed his images with thrusts of his pen, and sometimes his pipe, in the arena of a café table. When he became impassioned—crouching and twisting his hands that arthritis had turned into claws—and attempted to explain the sui generis figures and passes in his bullfight, one couldn't help seeing him as Mons had depicted him: a bearded minotaur swinging around to place the banderillas in his own back. A premonitory minotaur or perhaps merely a paraphrase of Stock's daring declaration: the painter—was he referring only to the tauromachian?—must be both bullfighter and bull. If not a matador, he had been a butcher's assistant in Düsseldorf during the lean years after the war, so that he could continue his studies in fine arts. The mere sight of certain slaughterhouse pieces by Rembrandt or Soutine, he asserted, still turned his stomach. And he was perplexed to discover that butchering a cow in a slaughterhouse is called a sacrifice in Spanish. Perhaps he saw himself, in that frightened bloodstained boy, as a priest still too much a novice to realize he had just taken part in a rite. Another little word, rite . . . that returned in a ritornel with a rictus of irritation. Certain images from the Düsseldorf slaughterhouse, permanently enveloped in the odor of blood, were more persistent in his memory, he explained, than any from the tauromachies of Goya and Picasso, which he never grew tired of admiring and even attempted to emulate.

The pass of the *verónica,* we suggested to him as a start: waiting motionless for the bull's charge—Mons unfurled Stock's Swedish newspaper—the cape extended between both hands. But Stock followed his own system and rules.

Look, he said, look how he grasps it (looking at the invisible poniard in his raised fist before adding: What do you call it? *Puntilla?*) when he's ready to deliver the final thrust, that's right, he said, nodding, and then he slammed his sharp, categorical fist down on the paper tablecloth covered with scrawls and rings of wine stains and looked again into the depths of his glass as if doubting it was empty, until his eyes glanced over at the befogged glass door and the swiftly moving nocturnal river of umbrellas and passing silhouettes on Potsdamer Strasse at five in the afternoon, which certainly must have struck him as terrible, and repeated in his Spanish: What do you call it? *Puntil-la?*

On that stormy, thundering all-saints boomsday we were back in the Café Strada—his favorite place in Berlin—and he was trying to explain to Mons for the first time the very rudimentary sketches, some improvised on the tablecloth, for the dreamlike or nightmarish tauromachy, *Oniromaquia* [*sic*], he called it, that had been obsessing him in recent weeks. He would begin at the end and, it seems, the *puntilla* would finish off or put the finishing touch to the first image of the first bull. The *puntilla* remedies the poor performance of the matador, he said punctiliously. The *puntilla* or the art of the coup de grâce, I thought I heard him mutter between his teeth, and again he clenched the invisible weapon in his fist.

Berlin is a good arena for a tauromachy, Mons pointed out with an engraver's dry pointed irony.

And especially the Café Strada . . . I tried to explain because neither one had heard of a bullfighter from the 1940s named Estrada.

Paradoxically, Stock had never gone to a bullfight despite the many years he had lived in Spain, principally in the fifties and sixties. His Spanish past was the origin of the tauromachy project. A young couple who were hairstylists had just converted their beauty salon on Knesebeckstrasse, Adamo & Ewa, into an art gallery. After a successful opening with a recently deceased and forgotten Russian post-suprematist painter who had anticipated the minimalists and the Fluxus movement, they were convinced the time was ripe for discovering the expatriate Stock. At first Stock had probably agreed to turn out bullfight sketches and engravings for reasons more pecuniary than painterly, though he did not totally disdain local Spanish color and would spice his conversation with Spanish exclamations and oaths accented with Teutonic rotundity.

We tried to give him a hand, and in the Café Strada we taught him the ABCs of the ambiguous vocabulary of bullfighting. It also struck Stock that almost all the words referring to the national fiesta had double meanings. *Corrida* denoted the bullfight, as well as an ejaculation. *Puntilla*, both the dagger's strike and lace. *Verdugo*, the sword that kills the bull in one thrust and the executioner of death sentences. *Muleta*, the cane that holds the killing cape and a crutch.

Mons continued his salon minitoreo—or café bullfighting (monitoreo?)—by attempting to execute the pass with the *muleta* called the *natural*, in which the red cloth on its cane is held in the left hand, Mons explained, without the help of the sword, in a form as natural as Stock extending his dexterous right hand to paint, until the bull is made to pass as close as possible. And we spent time in particular on the passes of the cape: the *larga,* or long pass; the *mariposa,* or butterfly; the *verónica,* and we insisted on this basic pass with the beautiful name of Veronica, the saintly woman who wiped the Holy Face and imprinted it on her veil . . . and at any moment we expected to see her walk into the Strada.

Stock was still clutching his sacrificial knife: Look, he had insisted, aspirating the K even more than usual, the *puntilla* grows in the fist, and between his index finger and thumb he made the mouthpiece of his pipe appear; the point of a sword . . . he added, again crashing his fist down on the table. *Herr Puntil-la* . . . should have been his nickname. The tip stiffens with death, he gushed, erect, almost eructate if it hits the mark. Was he risking a phallic fallacy? Despite our chauvinistic instruction, he wanted to paint a dance or ballet of death, he said, that would extend beyond a nation's folkloric circle. And then he began to ramble on about Abraham's sacrifice, the *Schachter,* he called him, and Jewish slaughterers or sacrificers, mixing *el toro* with the Torah, the cock or *gallo* of expiation with Rafael el Gallo, and the bull of Mithras— what a cult, enough to pull out of him an Olé Bull!—with the crucified burro in certain Roman graffiti, a gallimaufry ranging from *coq à l'âne,* surely culled from his hit-or-miss readings—a matador shows more method (we frequently saw him leafing through books in the small bookstore next to the Strada)—and from a recent nightmare. In the dark he could make out two hands, and in one—the right—the blade flared like a flame. In a flash he saw the points of two horns sharpened like nails. The sacrificial knife came to claim a victim and propitiate a terrible premonition. The *puntilla* that Stock proposed painting burst from the hilt in the fist in a torrent of blood.

## 2

N that stormy afternoon in the Strada perhaps he had already told us about the sacrificial bull, the crucified bull. The idea had come to him, he said, from a blackened board with two long nails protruding at the top like two horns, which he had picked out of a trash can in front of the Steinmetzstrasse market, near his house. He carried the *trouvée* bull's head to his room like a trophy, and sometimes, as if to demonstrate the utility of the ornament, or hornament, he would hang a jacket or his overcoat from the nails. By the nails of Christ! Another archaic Spanish expression he used from time to time. To heighten the resemblance to a bull's head, under the nails he painted—black on black—an inverted triangle. Straight-horned isosceles? The triangle or ménage à trois, perhaps, of tauromachy: bull, bullfighter, and death.

A disconcerted Mons followed Stock's illustrated explanations. Look, he said, scrawling on the tablecloth, the horns and head of the bull form a tau. (Tauromachian cross . . . ) And in a fury he drew lines on the paper trying to reproduce the confused image of the crucified figure (*Christoro?* he called it) that emerged from the tangled-skein labyrinth of his nightmare of a black bullring. Threads of a young black bull, strands of night. In the end everything was smudged, especially with red wine.

At that time he was drinking more than ever, and as he explained his wild tauromachy in tau, at a taurine five in the afternoon, he was on his third liter of wine. A half-liter carafe of Bordeaux every three quarters of an hour was his clepsydra. He spent his idle hours in the Strada, where solitude would not weigh as heavily as in the shabby room he rented in a ramshackle house of assignation behind Potsdamer Strasse. Perhaps that was where he met the little blond, almost an adolescent, who came to sit at his table in the Strada, in the back next to the plate-glass window, in the early afternoon. The corpulent bearded man with the wild white mane indoctrinating ad hoc the emaciated blond with lank hair hanging over her left eye and wearing an enigmatic half smile. Was she the Ariadne of the Minotaur-Christ? Or Veronica? He decided on Veronika—and it seemed to suit her—because of that veil of hair in the style of Veronica Lake. Though her name was really Ute. And the hair over her eye was not mere retrocopy or coquetry, as we would discover sometime later. She posed for Mons, with Stock's grudging permission, her hair gathered under a black top hat (a small snake in the center spray-painted in white) and her real left eye veiled by a cloud: *Nefertiti of Berlin*.

The fact that Veronika or Ute-Nefertiti was Mons's muse provoked—perhaps along with jealousy—a certain emulation in Stock. And she began to appear as an image or fragile icon in his barbaric tauromachy. And so, in a wash drawing, the slender bullfighter in white offers a toast by raising his inverted hat like a glass, inspired in the statue of Bacchus by Jacopo Sansovino (in Sansovino veritas!) and in the slim silhouette of Ute, stationed at her dangerous corner every night. This tauromachic, or taurobacchic, caprice contrasted with other more violent scenes, like the one in which the Maja-Veronika with her hair veiling her face and wearing a high Spanish comb attempted to repel or seize by the horns the bull half-raised over the front rows of seats in the bull-ring.

# 3

THE café table was the center of Stock's universe, and he almost never left it except to cross the street to buy a newspaper from Göteborg (in which his only daughter published a financial column that he read with more devotion than comprehension) or to look for a book in the bookstore next door, which he would copiously underline. And when it was very late, when he was hoping perhaps to see Ute, he would take up his post at the foot of the Türkischer Basar or in some *Imbiss* in the area to keep watch over the night from his high stool and pretend to eat with good appetite his inedible sausage. But he would return, disappointed, to his fixed place in the Strada to wait for closing time and then close himself off, alone in his wretched room.

Look, his cane, when on another night he showed us the *muleta* and the bull or, more accurately, the bull on crutches that came into the arena limping, falling from time to time, too harshly chastised by the picador or perhaps by sandbags hurled among shouts and whistles, until a chest pass, in a graphic gesture of Stock's left hand—he had begun to learn the rudiments of the fiesta—lifted up the crippled bull on those useful supports. When maimed I make my move . . . said Mons, but I don't believe Stock caught the reference, best foot forward for a bull that charges on crutches.

Caught on the horns of too many images, a melange of *muletas,* canes, and crutches, taurine orthopedics. And a long et cetera of tentative epithets testing the spirit. Stock seemed pleased to see that he had impressed—or at least surprised— us with so lame an image of surrender. And faced with that crippled bull, heh? I would finally realize that I had first seen Veronika with the hanging hair many nights ago on the corner of the Ku'damm and Uhlandstrasse, leading a crippled man of advanced years gently and affectionately by the arm (and it was that solicitude, she in her white ski outfit, leaning deferentially toward the little man in the dark raincoat, that attracted my interest) and helping him climb the carpeted stairs of that house lit by the neon sign of the restaurant Papillon and a mutilated *Ein bit bitte!*—an invitation that could lead us to a butterfly pass on which death sometimes alights. Slow *muletas,* at last the lethal *muleta* in order to advance toward death in the supreme instant that lengthens into a moment of truth. And while the painter offered his *muleta* metaphor, he rested his armpit on the back of his chair, ready to expound on the irresistible charge of the bull on crutches.

# 4

STOCK accumulated associations in his baroque van Gogh–Goyesque bullfight. During the van Gogh phase he continually clutched in his clawed hand a volume of van Gogh's letters to his brother Theo as if it were his prayer book. It was also in a sense his *Summa Theologica*. Listen to what he tells Theo: In my work I risk my life and my reason . . . He underlined countless passages in ink. He wrote notes and comments in the margins. And sometimes he even exclaimed: "Bravo Vincent!" "Vincent convinces!" He maintained, half seriously, that van Gogh cut off his ear in a bullfighter's passionate outburst of bravura and generosity, a tauromachian imitation. If a bull's ear is the reward given for a bullfighter's excellent performance, the painter— who in the arena of his blank canvas is both bullfighter and bull—rewarded his own performance by demonstrating the daring of his passes. In that case, Mons said, van Gogh should have cut off both his ears. Not to mention his tail . . . But Stock insisted that van Gogh cut off his ear because of a tauromachian influence or mimesis. And he thought it significant that in the month of December 1888, when van Gogh cut off his ear in Arles, he also painted a tauromachy, *Les Arènes d'Arles,* that now hangs in the Hermitage in Saint Petersburg. The mutilated ear was, he believed, both offering and sacrifice. Which is why he offered it to Rachel, a prostitute and perhaps his only friend in Arles. As if it were pure gold. Washed and wrapped in a handkerchief. Which did not prevent Rachel from falling into a faint upon seeing that Christmas present.

During this time a macabre article in the Berlin papers heightened Stock's obsession: a Serb immigrant was arrested by the German police when, in the Nollendorfplatz flea market, he tried to sell human ears, presumably from Bosnian victims, made into amulets and key chains. For forty marks each.

Stock was prepared to pardon Dr. Félix Rey, who had treated the dis-eared painter in the hospital at Arles and for years had used the portrait that van Gogh painted of him to cover a hole in his henhouse (it is now in the Push-kin Museum in Moscow) because the good doctor kept his patient's ear, or piece of ear, in a jar. Unfortunately, some months later, an assistant threw the historic relic into the trash.

Stock sketched an ear in a flask (was he trying to restore it?) that looked more like a fetus curled into a ball. No doubt his obsession was gestating.

One afternoon late in December he appeared in the Strada with a bandage covering his right temple and ear. With the bandage and his pipe, it was clear he was trying to copy one of van Gogh's self-portraits. Undoubtedly painted in front of the mirror, because the painter had really cut off the lobe of his left ear. The left?! Stock expressed his aston-ishment with a pained expression. The error or inexactitude must have mortified him. Stock bore the jibes stoically and said, without attributing too much importance to it, that last night, in the early hours, he had found himself involved involuntarily in a fight in a dive on Potsdamer Strasse. Ute-Veronika, who came to Mons's studio from time to time, confirmed the story of the fight but added the epilogue: When she had attempted to cut some strips of cloth to ban-dage him, Stock had pulled the scissors out of her hand and tried to cut off his battered ear. Luckily, he had been so drunk that he had barely inflicted a few superficial cuts. His ear as a medium of exchange? As a substitute for another token, one of the most painful kinds?

Stock's tauromachia underwent a metamorphosis with touches and sword thrusts both esthetic and mythic. He penetrated another arena of his bullfight, following the bull with the golden balls, as he called it, the bull-scrotum transformed into the bag of life. Two stiff pricks sprouted from the forehead of this horny minotaur. He did not need to turn to mythology or mere biology (how many Pasiphaës and Europas, how many bacchantes could a good bull cover?) in order to represent in suggestive taurography the beast that is the incarnation of virility and sexual potency. You have to grab this bull by his balled horns, and he smiled as he glanced malevolently at Veronika, who probably was not familiar with the expression. The horns of plenty, one might add, if not for the fact that this hyperballic bull was like an incongruous apparition, perhaps the phantom of a feared castration. A cloak-and-dagger melodrama?

# 5

To wear the world as your bullfighter's hat, your *montera* . . . —or was he saying "mount"?—and radiant, verbose, he raised his hands to his large head as if he were going to cap the terrestrial sphere before setting out on a cosmic stroll. And he pointed out that he had spent his honeymoon (more than thirty years ago) in a *pensión* on the calle de la Montera in Madrid. And had painted Karen nude, sitting on the edge of the bed, wearing only a bullfighter's hat. This *montera,* purchased in the Rastro, inspired other, more daring bullfighting poses for his new bride. When their money ran out, he stationed himself outside the Prado Museum to sell the drawings. Stock soon realized that the drawings sold much more quickly if his wife-model was with him so that buyers could appreciate the resemblance. Until those passes or poses scandalized some orthodox afi-cionados and the painter and his model found themselves in the nearest commissary of police. Stock laughed when he recalled his first tauromachian steps or missteps, his blood wedding of sangría and sand. His marriage had ended barely a year before, principally because of his drinking, he said. But the memory of their happy years in Spain, the south of France, and Sweden (the country of his wife and daughter) could not separate him from the bottle. On the contrary, sometimes by five in the afternoon he found it difficult to articulate words with his stumbling tongue. And his dis-putes with Ute turned increasingly violent. Bottle ends in battle . . . One night he had a spectacular fall down the stairs in his house. From then on his limp became more and more pronounced and *muletas* reappeared almost obsessively in his sketches. The bullfighter's *montera* rested on the *muleta*. Two crossed *muletas* became an unsettling enigma. The X of his psyche? The crossroads or *via crucis* of his own bullfight?

# 6

CROSS potent potentialized by *muletas*. No doubt he had in mind that a cross potent in German includes the word crutches, *Krücken*, before the cross: *Krückenkreuz*. The obsession with the cross in his painting. *In hoc signo* . . . Berlin is a great cemetery, and he pointed at the rows of white crosses on dark windows one night when we were walking in Kreuzberg. And immediately described the vision of the black bull that stormed out of the bull pen and opened into a cross when it charged. Now and in the moment of truth . . . the sword buried all the way to the crosspiece (or ball) and the bull transformed into a hurled weapon, blood gushing from dark vein or piercing blade, the back of the neck star-crossed, and the bull collapsed, crucified. He lengthened and extended the cross, staring fixedly at his black beast. He gesticulated over the sketches and even made smudges like blood stains. That encrusted cross potent became crucial to the bloody sacrifice of the emissary beast. *Porca miseria!* He laughed so as not to take his tauromachy too seriously. Again he crossed out and revised the confusing muddle. Enough, the line can't be crossed, an impenetrable tangle all around. The victim transformed, finally, into the weapon of his own sacrifice. This vision of the bull-cross, sharp as a sword, appeared after a fight with Ute in which she had defended herself and threatened him with her dressmaker's shears. *Schere-razade* . . . Was she capable of killing? And he shook his head in disbelief. But, he added, murder is at times a distorted suicide, premeditated and treacherous. We weren't sure we followed very well, though we tried to accommodate ourselves to his capricious limping pace. The pass of the black cross (or perhaps he said mass), he murmured, rolling his eyes, at the crossroads of Yorckstrasse and Mehringdamm. And the bull cross of his tangled vision became more and more deeply encrusted.

Misfortunes and falls from grace—like the Graces—never come singly, and soon after his fall down the stairs Stock began to suffer pains and vision problems in his right eye. He didn't know whether to attribute this to his fall or his fight in the gambling den. It worried him even more because he had blurred vision in his left eye. The right one does the work of two, he once said with a wink. Fearing the worst, he tried sketching with his eyes closed. Or scribbling, because he confused the lines. He was dumbfounded by the dexterity of Mons, who, with closed eyes, drew him in four strokes on the tablecloth at the Strada. The Minotaur Stock leaning on his cane-sword . . . But Stock, whose griefs and drinking were on the rise, was in no mood for caricatures. He went to Dr. Vollender, a former schoolmate (his ophthalmological consulting room, in a faded building in Halensee, was decorated with early works by Stock that filled him with embarrassment and nostalgia: *Sunset in Villa Kügel, Potato Eaters in Essen, Burial of the Miner* . . . ) whose diagnosis was an inflammation of the iris probably caused by arthritis. The terminology (inflammation of the uveal tunica) seemed particularly intimidating to him.

Medical treatment alleviated the pain but not the anguish, which was manifested as wounds like eyes on the bodies of bulls, bullfighters, and picadors. The bullring was a great inflamed eye, the bullfighter with his cape and the bull— joined by two ink stains—forming the pupil.

The eyes were torn at times, curved into horns and stars. The horns of the moon . . . Waning and waxing, above and below, as if reflected in black water. Perhaps he had in mind the story Mons had told him of the boy who was a novice bullfighter and at night would swim across the Guadalquivir to separate a bull from the herd that grazed and took their ease in a field of stars. Fighting the bull naked was a nascent way of closing distances. His left hand holds the damp shirt (or was it his cap?) like a *muleta* in a natural pass. Stock no longer confused it with the chest pass. Horn-handled knives, half-moon scimitars, almost touch the slender chest as they speed by, scythes that reap the night. And in the inky river the sharpened horns of the moon glint and eddy. Picturesque bull horns budding for an oneiric tauromachy.

Closing/conciliating distances: his way of brandishing the brush, the palette knife, the pencil . . . and sighting over them as if they were weapons reminded me of Mons narrowing his eyes aggressively as he stood in front of the canvas. Painting as tauromachy—which is what Stock also thought. Paintorero, if not braggartist. Danger in every detail. Danger always made him think of his father, a miner. He could still hear the staccato of his cough. He had died with the satisfaction of knowing his son would not go down to the mines. Though Stock's course of study had disappointed him: industrial draftsman was not a title like the one his friend Vollender had. Each profession has its dangers, Stock believed, and he was prepared to face his.

Stock with his bible of van Gogh in Golgotha: I risk my life and my reason . . . Reason? To know how to risk, to take a risk. Expose and expound . . . Perhaps Stock had accepted the charge of that tauromachy as an invitation to return to the arena, to the danger of each day's labor, its *faena*. *Faena* . . . another two-edged bullfighting term. He hadn't painted for months. Only sketches and drawings. Tauromockeries. Tauromackerels . . . I don't paint anything here, he would say, and drain his glass of wine.

After twenty years in Sweden he had returned to his own country a complete stranger. And nothing remained of the Berlin of his youth. Gone like the Wall. And while he looked or pretended to look for a studio, he could while away the hours of his insomnia in his wretched little room imagining his tauromachy of bulls and gold, *el toro* and *el oro*, that he sometimes called "auromachy" as if it were an alchemical work. During this time he exchanged the van Gogh book for one by Jung on alchemy, and he became interested in the concept of the "great work" (Stock, in his eternal black leather smock, had the look of a crazed alchemist) and concluded this could not be achieved unless preceded by destruction and metamorphosis. *Mets ta mort fausse,* he said in fairly good French as he looked at his glass of French wine. Or was he sounding out metamorphose? We weren't sure we had understood him and Mons brought him back to the terrain of risk and his signature saint, van Gogh, who seemed to have lost his halo. Stock had not lost his devotion to him but claimed, in all seriousness, that the Dutchman had cheated with his ear. He had given, he said, an ear for an eye . . . For a painter, losing an ear represents no risk at all. Nobody, in fact, paints by ear. For a real painter it was easier to lose his reason—and even his life—than his sight . . . Stock concluded impassively.

Every evening Ute thought him even stranger, perhaps because of the pains in his eye, and she began to fear him. Especially, she told Mons, late one night when she found him sitting on the bed and repeating like one possessed sacrifice, sacrifice, sacrifice . . . Without sacrifice there is no art was his *muletilla,* his motto. And he continued to repeat "sacrifice" until he finally saw Ute, naked and terrified, in front of him.

On another night a car almost ran him down on Potsdamer Strasse. The few witnesses declared that it was he who had hurled himself at the car, shaking his overcoat in both hands. A *verónica?* Cape swirling over the hood . . . Perhaps the speeding car looked to him like a bull.

He continued to explain his tauromachy to us in the Strada, but the artful passes and figures had become more schematic and geometric. Vision problems? we wondered. Painting is mental, Mons correctly recalled. The cornupete triangle repeated like a leitmotiv. The inverted delta of death. Dagger of Damocles. Triangle with a hidden mystery? The black triangle he had painted on his horned board. He had set his board-bull on the table, against the wall, and Ute told us that on many nights she found him sitting and staring at it or into it as if it were a mirror. Stock said the pains in his eye did not let him sleep and poured himself another glass of brandy.

Articles in various German newspapers and magazines that attempted to reconstruct, not always in very reliable ways, what occurred a short while later, in the small hours of another night, forcefully called attention to Stock and his bullfight in Berlin. The testimony of Ute-Veronika was important a posteriori, because when she came to Stock's room the terrible event had already taken place. Stock was unconscious and covered in blood. There was blood on the sheets, the towels, the quilt, the rug, the walls. Stock had drunk too much, trying to ease his pain, and he could not recall exactly what had happened. Whether he had tripped and fallen against the board-bull, piercing his eyes with the nails or, what was more likely, according to the hypothesis of the Berlin magazine *Zitty*, he had thrown himself in a frenzy onto the nails he had mistaken for horns. I'll never be able to hear the phrase "piercing eyes" in the same way again, Mons said.

The gallery owners Adamo and Ewa immediately took charge of Stock, who fortunately lost only the eye with blurred vision though the problems in his right eye remained serious. And they contributed, with the help of the doctors, to the metamorphosis of Stock. Perhaps they also brought their experience as stylists to the process of transformation. With great fanfare the tauromachian exhibit was announced two months later. In the center of the former beauty salon on Knesebeckstrasse they arranged a white ring like a bullfight arena, recalling the one in the Beuys retrospective at the Gropius-Bau. And Adamo and Ewa had placed scraps of bloodstained sheets and towels alongside taurine drawings and sketches, most of them bloodstained too, in a series of boxes with glass lids, like reliquaries, as if these were the *burladeros* where bullfighters take refuge. And in the center of the ring or amphitheater, Stock's bullfight retable: the bloodstained board with the horn-nails and black triangle. But the most surprising element was Stock himself. He was unrecognizable at the opening. Wearing a black twill suit and dark glasses, clean-shaven, his hair pulled back in a ponytail like the *coleta* of a bullfighter, tapping his chest with a fan, smiling, perfectly sober, he circulated with ability and agility among wineglasses, shoulders, and décolleté necklines, accepting kisses, pats on the back, and congratulations. The rumor had spread, even before the opening of his show, that several museums were bidding for the "board-bull" of the sacrifice. Stock's stock is finally up, I heard a bony woman say in English; she was later introduced to me as the artist's daughter. And Stock, in one of the few moments when he did not have to use his fan in a crowd of fans and aficionados, gave me, very seriously, this message for Mons: One must murder the martyr that every artist carries inside.

# IX

# With
# Bouvard and Pécuchet
# in Cyberspace

I N this part we ought to view ourselves in
the third person in order to better follow our
couple, I was saying to Mons on the boulevard
Bourdon at the very moment when a very different pairing
came along to divert our attention to other courses of
action.

That one down there, said Emil Alia, and Mons pointed
his pencil at the contorted couple endlessly exchanging
kisses beside the barges on the Canal Saint-Martin, yes, those
turtledoves with torticollis, he insisted, perhaps they don't
know that sometimes there are communicative kisses, from
life to literature and vice versa, and in moments like this of
osmosis-rapture-fascination, whatever you call it, those two
mouth-to-mouthers are now also Horacio and Lucia, say,
and let's call them by name, those Rioplatensean lovers
along the Seine who also had their Bouvard and Pécuchet
side, *che*, and come back from chapter or square 21 of their
*Hopscotch* to exalt with a kiss the free life of Paris and, perhaps without suspecting it, literature too, in what may be
involuntary homage to their ancestors, Flaubert's two copyists, who met for the first time along this same canal of ink-
colored water. But the stale theory that life imitates or limits
art did not please Mons, for whom art limits life and its
superfluous redundancies and excesses, and he reduced

the closely embracing couple below us to an obscure Chinese scrawl or gleeful hieroglyph on his drawing paper and seemed more interested in the boats moored at the docks along the canal, which he was copying along with their names: *Andromède,* the name of a constellation and before that of the wife of Perseus, Emil the mythologer personified, and by a terrible coincidence on the opposite bank there was a tender called *Méduse,* who also lost her head because of Perseus, he persisted, and it is above all the name of a raft, see Géricault's in the Louvre, and he specified that Géricault was born in Rouen like Flaubert and—another coincidence—in the same year, 1791, as Bouvard and Pécuchet; but Mons's nimble pencil was already sketching a black barge named *Swan,* its S as graceful as the bird, and then the admirer of Flaubert could not help but remark that the swan song of the bard of Croisset was his posthumous, unfinished, and unfinishable novel, *Bouvard and Pécuchet,* a farcical critical encyclopedia, its author called it, a kind of human encyclomediocrity of knowledge, of ignorance that is unconscious and invincible, at which point Mons energetically shelved the matter, declaring the sketch and the disquisition concluded.

On the boulevard Bourdon, under an almost summery April sun, Emil returned to his old tricks and ventured the guess that perhaps Flaubert chose to open his encyclopedia and interminable epic about writing with this boulevard whose name comes from typographical terminology—*bourdon,* a typesetter's omission—and Mons, less attached to letters than to images, observed that their shadows—the bulky one cast by a hulking Mons, the human mountain, and Emil's filiform silhouette—reproduced *in grosso modo* the fig-

N this part we ought to view ourselves in
the third person in order to better follow our
couple, I was saying to Mons on the boulevard
Bourdon at the very moment when a very different pairing
came along to divert our attention to other courses of
action.

That one down there, said Emil Alia, and Mons pointed
his pencil at the contorted couple endlessly exchanging
kisses beside the barges on the Canal Saint-Martin, yes, those
turtledoves with torticollis, he insisted, perhaps they don't
know that sometimes there are communicative kisses, from
life to literature and vice versa, and in moments like this of
osmosis-rapture-fascination, whatever you call it, those two
mouth-to-mouthers are now also Horacio and Lucia, say,
and let's call them by name, those Rioplatensean lovers
along the Seine who also had their Bouvard and Pécuchet
side, *che,* and come back from chapter or square 21 of their
*Hopscotch* to exalt with a kiss the free life of Paris and, perhaps without suspecting it, literature too, in what may be
involuntary homage to their ancestors, Flaubert's two copyists, who met for the first time along this same canal of ink-
colored water. But the stale theory that life imitates or limits
art did not please Mons, for whom art limits life and its
superfluous redundancies and excesses, and he reduced

the closely embracing couple below us to an obscure
Chinese scrawl or gleeful hieroglyph on his drawing paper
and seemed more interested in the boats moored at the
docks along the canal, which he was copying along with
their names: *Andromède*, the name of a constellation and
before that of the wife of Perseus, Emil the mythologer
personified, and by a terrible coincidence on the opposite
bank there was a tender called *Méduse*, who also lost her
head because of Perseus, he persisted, and it is above all the
name of a raft, see Géricault's in the Louvre, and he specified that Géricault was born in Rouen like Flaubert and—
another coincidence—in the same year, 1791, as Bouvard and
Pécuchet; but Mons's nimble pencil was already sketching a
black barge named *Swan*, its S as graceful as the bird, and
then the admirer of Flaubert could not help but remark that
the swan song of the bard of Croisset was his posthumous,
unfinished, and unfinishable novel, *Bouvard and Pécuchet*, a
farcical critical encyclopedia, its author called it, a kind of
human encyclomediocrity of knowledge, of ignorance that
is unconscious and invincible, at which point Mons energetically shelved the matter, declaring the sketch and the disquisition concluded.

On the boulevard Bourdon, under an almost summery
April sun, Emil returned to his old tricks and ventured the
guess that perhaps Flaubert chose to open his encyclopedia
and interminable epic about writing with this boulevard
whose name comes from typographical terminology—
*bourdon*, a typesetter's omission—and Mons, less attached to
letters than to images, observed that their shadows—the
bulky one cast by a hulking Mons, the human mountain, and
Emil's filiform silhouette—reproduced *in grosso modo* the fig-

ures of Bouvard and Pécuchet. Though Mons's egg-head lacked Bouvard's blond ringlets, and he—Mons did not overlook this—did not mince along like Pécuchet.

Mons had portrayed Bouvard as a red-faced, big-bellied man with an air part roguish, part Rabelaisian—it was no accident that his name was also François—and half-closed blue eyes in a round, rather childish face. And Pécuchet as small and dark, the half-moon of his visored cap over his eyes, a nose almost as long as his face, a limp mustache, and thin hair plastered to his temples like a wig. Mons had given them the incongruous appearance of middle-aged adolescents. He had painted them at the age they were, forty-six, when they met on that hot Sunday in August on the boulevard Bourdon. Meteorology, not chronology, opens *Bouvard and Pécuchet,* an anticyclonic Emil had pointed out to him. Curiously, Robert Musil's *The Man Without Qualities,* that brief chronicle of the end of an empire and an epoch, Bouvardpécuchesque in so many ways, also begins meteorologically. Moreover, both hypernovels begin in August, which is the month most . . . and he stopped abruptly when he saw Mons walking toward a bench. They begin in August, he went on, but don't ever end . . .

Though the sun of that April first could not compare to the one that shone during the dog days, he recalled that on this very bench, in the shade of a tall tree, in the middle of boulevard Bourdon, he had sat, torpid, on a Sunday afternoon in August when the thermometer reached exactly thirty-three degrees Centigrade and asked himself, then as now, if this could be the same bench where Bouvard and Pécuchet had met when they both sat down at the same moment. Mons, however, would rather have known if in

1838, when the two copyists met, the benches along boulevard Bourdon were also painted green.

The sun would make the layer of dust glisten . . . Emil suggested. How observant! Mons cut him off drily.

At dusk they returned to the boulevard Bourdon and again approached the Canal Saint-Martin (the water was now the color of India ink, or night) and Mons thought he saw *Yvetot,* in white letters, on the prow of a barge as black as a coffin that was moving toward the Bastille. An evil omen? The chronologist said that the taking of the Bastille occurred only two years before the birth of Bouvard and Pécuchet, and perhaps that was why they attempted to determine the causes of the Revolution.

When he was preparing the *Illustrated Encyclopedia of Bouvard and Pécuchet* with Mons, he recalled, they would frequently go together to the Parisian places associated with the two peerless copyists. Their pilgrimage to the sites of the geniuses should have ended with a visit to the town to which the two Parisian natives retired, Chavignolles, between Caen and Falaise in Calvados, but the excursion was always postponed.

In the Saint-Cloud flea market Mons had found a faded photograph of the countryside, which he copied in duplicate, as if for a stereoscopic viewer, because he thought it corresponded to the panorama that Bouvard and Pécuchet might have contemplated from their house in Chavignolles: fields stretching to the horizon, to the right a barn and a church steeple, to the left a row of poplar trees.

It is likely that this double view reminded Mons of the one he contemplated from the windows of his studio in

Enfer: the fields, the farm of Madame Pierret, the line of birches along the horizon.

They went to the Louvre to find the Raphael that the copyists pretended to love, and after hesitating between the portrait of Baldassare Castiglione, the greatest courtier in the world, and Saint George slaying the dragon, they finally stood before the statue of the seated *Scribe*. They agreed that Bouvard would have known how to adopt the pose of his Egyptian colleague.

On the rue Saint-Martin, Mons recognized the garret— though the building's facade had been modernized—where he had lived and painted for a few months many years earlier, before they had raised the intestinal tubes of the nearby Pompidou Center. In that room with dormer windows and yellowish walls, he had discovered, inscribed or scratched into a plaster column of the blocked-up fireplace, the name Pécuchet, the P and T in tall strokes. Who could have engraved it? Some student? The mystery of the yellow room.

Mons also recalled his years as the king of bohemia on the rue des Écoles when we passed the Collège de France, where he had attended courses in Sanskrit—and Arabic, like Bouvard and Pécuchet—only to keep warm during that severe winter when he didn't have a cent.

One snowy night, as he skidded along the narrow rue Hautefeuille toward the boulevard Saint-Germain, he saw or tried to see a high leaf that Bouvard had covered with his rounded handwriting when he worked in the firm of Descambos Brothers, Alsatian Textiles, at number 92.

Another night, on the rue Saint-Denis, they bouvardized the streetwalkers with audacious reciprovocations that would have made the timid Pécuchet blush.

Bouncing breasts overflowing their necklines looked like balloons to Mons. He was seeing everything now through the eyes of the master copyists.

He had the idea of locking himself away on his farm in Enfer along with his accomplice, the two of them isolated in order to work on the monumental encyclopedia in syntony with the two retirees of Chavignolles. The descent to the chemin d'Avernes is easy . . . a well-disposed Emil joked. Mons the illustrator had begun his work at the end, with the absurditary, and was preparing, in no particular order and in concert with the commentator, a series of vignettes to which the annotator would add footnotes as swift as those of Achilles:

A soot-covered chimney sweep in a patched swallow-tailed coat, tails flying in the wind like a swallow's wings, pedaled a bicycle over the legend: One chimney sweep does not the winter make.

A pack of Camels with a desert landscape and ruminant over the captious question: Camel or dromedary?

A burning candle that illuminated the exclamation *Fiat lux!*

A replica of the bust of Nefertiti in the Egyptian Museum of Berlin (her left eye vacant) with the title in French: *Un Dessert sans fromage.*

The Parisian preparations for the *Illustrated Encyclopedia of Bouvard and Pécuchet* took longer than expected—like Roman public works or pharaonic pyramids—and Mons had to return to Berlin to conclude a mural project on the van-

ished Wall. But from Paris his collaborator sent him punc-
tual reports and kept him abreast of events. Events, indeed:
Bouvard and Pécuchet live and I've found them on the Internet! Emil informed him with an exclamation point.

Out of curiosity he had gone into a cybercafé across from
the Luxembourg Garden on the rue Médicis, frequented
by Americans in particular who went in to receive and
send e-mail, and at the bar he found a pile of brochures in
which the two indefatigable copyists announced themselves:
http://www.bouvardetpecuchet.fr. The three Ws repeated
like a slogan or the postscript to a hamletter at the end of the
brochure: Words, Words, Words . . . Only connect!

He sat down at the first free monitor and did not take
very long to find them on the screen, with the help of the
obliging wasp-waisted cyberwaitress—he did not fail to
specify this to Mons—whose name turned out to be Melissa,
which he would have preferred to shorten to Mélie, like the
Norman servant girl who deflowered the fifty-year-old
Pécuchet, with gonorrhea as punishment or penitence, free
of charge.

Click, click, the mouse as nervous as a library rat, and in
the blue of cyberspace the two cybercopyists suddenly came
into view. They appeared first in a color photograph, he
informed Mons, looking just as he had portrayed them, so
precisely and presciently, in his imaginary portrait. Though
Pécuchet now wore a baseball cap that did not go very
well with his old monk's habit. A copyist monk, like those
who from their monastic writing tables preserved culture
with Benedictine patience during the Middle Ages. Though
at times, as they were copying, their hands slipped and

emended or appended according to the mandates of their holy order.

Both of them, Bouvard and Pécuchet, had settled into a perpetually immature maturity, like fifty-year-old Peter Pans. Both were fiftyish, like Don Quixote, as seen so clearly by Borges, who also observed with his habitual clairvoyance that Flaubert's two copyists are outside time in an eternity that is the ideal space for writing forever recommenced, the perpetual clean slate of an unending two-handed game in which time does not pass for those two clerks condemned to write signs and symbols, world without end.

At his death Flaubert the Master, or rather lord and master, the *Maître,* in short, of Bouvard and Pécuchet, left his summary of scraps, his encyclopedia and varied calvary of miscellaneous rewritings, unfinished, so that the two copyists would not die but relieve and reveal him through their senseless passion. Flaubert, who so often referred to the foolishness of wanting to conclude, is proof that in literature nothing is really begun and nothing ended, that everything is transformed and continued. The great irony is that Flaubert copied an insignificant little story, "The Two Scribes," by an obscure author, which was transformed into his Monument with a capital M: the endless copying of two seekers of wisdom who ended up clutching at the life raft of their desks, the materiality of their downstrokes.

The two copyists heard their master's voice, his final order: *Copy.* Nothing more and nothing less. Not "as before," as Flaubert's niece later added after the word *Copy,* fraudulently expanding the mandate. *Copy,* a categorical command. Bouvard and Pécuchet were, as they say, programmed.

In the plan left by Flaubert he indicates that the two copy-

ists order a double writing desk from a carpenter in Chavignolles.

According to the report that Mons received in Berlin,
this double desk was transformed into a double monitor—
scientific progress, et cetera . . . —at which Bouvard and
Pécuchet navigate cyberspace without leaving their Norman village, in order to go against the tide and propagate
creative forms of writing—those species threatened with
extinction—in every direction.

Let us focus first on prose, they proposed.

In the posthumous plan left by their master Flaubert, it
was twice indicated that the two copyists were concerned
with the "Future of Literature." Pécuchet saw it as grim.
Disseminating good literature, Bouvard believed, was a
way of saving it. And therefore they took advantage of the
Net's possibilities. Let us go on the Internet, inside the Tro-
jan horse, Bouvard proposed, and introduce true writing—
the real thing—into the enemy citadel of simulacra and
virtuality.

The unfathomable emptiness of infinite cyberspace terri-
fies me, Pécuchet freely pontificated. Bouvard maintained
that they could find no better space to present and preserve
works censored or suppressed by censorship. Pécuchet stressed
that in our day the greatest censorship lies in rampant com-
mercialism, which not only does not permit the birth and
growth of novels that ensure the renovation and perpetua-
tion of the genre, for example, but substitutes its own cuckoo
eggs and passes them off as literature. Bouvard maintained
that there was no time or space to lose and proposed scan-
ning meritorious novels that were out of print or forgotten
or worthy of being promoted as exemplary. Pécuchet re-

jected the scanner and preferred to type in the chosen books letter by letter, because he wanted to preach by example: the man who writes reads twice.

Their criterion for selection primarily excluded those novels that say what can be said by other means and were in reality poor imitations, between covers, of film or television. Bouvard at times was overindulgent and proposed copying rather dispensable books, but Pécuchet, like his American colleague Bartleby, would cut him off with a curt "I would prefer not."

On subsequent visits to the cybercafé on the rue Médicis, the neo-internaut—assisted by Melissa, now called Mélie—made increasingly frequent contact with the two copyists from Chavignolles.

The hypertext exists, but for the moment it is in the text, Pécuchet claimed, in the great texts of literature.

A line by Joyce, Proust, or Kafka, no matter how short, never ends. In the pages of these writers and other true creators, windows are opened to the infinite, he proclaimed.

Not to mention other even older classics. For instance Cervantes, first and last, a plural author. And more complex with every passing year.

Using the Pierre Menard system, they devotedly copied *Don Quixote,* the book of origins, they recognized at once.

Questioned by the neointernaut regarding the contemporary Spanish novel, they confessed they knew little about it but intended to bring themselves up to date with the latest thing at the earliest moment.

In their library at Chavignolles they found a *History of Contemporary Spanish Literature,* dated 1878, the author's name nothing less than Gustave, Gustave Hubbard, and when they leafed through the book they discovered that Spaniards of the time, in the midst of a full-blown political and economic crisis, had thrown themselves avidly into the reading of romantic cloak-and-dagger novels by a certain Fernández y González, called the Spanish Dumas. But no doubt matters have changed a great deal since then, Bouvard concluded.

Pécuchet had heard that many translations were published in Spain, many translations of everything, especially novels—including a good many bad novels that were sometimes imitated with great success—but he could not understand why great translations had been out of print for so long, such as *The Devil to Pay in the Backlands,* by the Brazilian Guimarães Rosa, or *That Awful Mess on Via Merulana,* by the Italian Carlo Emilio Gadda, books that they were prepared to disseminate on the Internet. As soon as they finished copying Cocteau's *Le Potomak,* which was unavailable in France, Bouvard added.

In recent months they had followed in fascination the lapses—relapses, rather—in the cross-country career of a confidence man named Foureau, who had created an enterprise, in reality a monumental swindle, called "La vie de château," which organized festivals, medieval feasts, fancy parties and even rap soirées in various French palaces and "châteaux," principally in the Île-de-France. The mansions and palaces existed, but their owners (who never received the promised generous rental fee) were gulled almost as much as the gullible people who had paid for festivals and feasts that never took place.

This Monsieur Foureau was probably a descendant, Pécuchet suspected, of that mayor, *l'échevin!* . . . who had

given them so many headaches because he had the inso-
lence to claim for himself a manor house—*une manière de
château*—and a thirty-eight-hectare farm in Chavignolles,
and gave as a reference a nonexistent address in Paris: 46, rue
Simon Crubellier, 3d rt., in the seventeenth arrondissement.

Bouvard had already opened a file entitled *Monsieur Foureau,* which, he believed, might eventually become a picaresque
novel.

They also edited the town newsletter and had created
another site on the Internet, *Chavignolles: Notre village,* where
they gathered local news and information along with a series
of banners unfurled to their own creativity and that of their
neighbors. They were also planning to open a site on the net
called SITE, for writing verses. But for the moment they
were engaged in prose, which is easier to do than verse.

The neo-internaut eventually asked if they didn't feel
trapped in the circular ruins of a cyclopean encyclopedia.
When he finished typing the question he became aware of
the error; he had written *runes, runes* phosphorescing on the
screen and at the same time sowing the doubt that perhaps
another copyist, at another monitor, was monitoring and
questioning the erroneous query he had just formulated. He
decided then to end the session—tomorrow was another
day—and propose to Mélie a stroll along the Canal Saint-
Martin, following Mons's suggestion from Berlin. That he
lead her to water, O Mélie! Enough chatter. Mélie and Emil,
*méli-mélo,* in the end a cuddly muddle that brought them
happily back to the beginning.

# X

# Mons in Enfer

# I

# Monster Pieces

## (PICTURES AT AN EXHIBITION)

# I

# Mons . . .

ONS . . . Mons . . . Monster! They chased him, screaming and throwing stones. An afternoon of harassment after he broke through the surrounding circle (closer and closer the chorus of howling monkeys) and raced across the soccer field that must have once been a cemetery because sometimes they found bones there and even an occasional skull that still had its hair. His legs were too long for his ten years, and with his scabby shaved head and perpetually staring eyes, his classmates at boarding school found him as strange as his last name. And could barely understand his broken, limited Spanish. Monster? Alone in the freezing washroom, he inspected in profile the gash on his cheekbone. Was he turning the other cheek? Squeezing the tube of toothpaste onto the mirror, he began to paint his first self-portrait over unattainable features. Half a century later he repeated the gesture in his studio at Enfer, squeezing the tube of cadmium white onto the canvas, confirming that now, as then, his hidden face was unattainable.

## 2

# Another Teratological Portrait

Y ou? The painter Basil Hallward hesitated as he was about to give the final brush stroke to his *Picture of Dorian Gray,* peering into it as if it were a mirror and an abyss, fascinated to recognize himself in the depths of that brilliant surface, though the features were so different from his own, which were much less correct; and as he attempted to rectify with that last touch of the brush a tiny wrinkle on the throat, he suddenly felt on his own neck the murderous knife of Dorian Gray, who, after slitting his throat without ceremony or explanation, also slashed his own masterpiece, rending the veil that separates art from life, or death, the winding sheet that joined them both, model and artist, in identical cadaverous rigidity, and the stony features and beautiful composition would be destroyed; his portrait of Dorian Gray, the degenerate hedonistic Adonis, was in reality his secret portrait of the artist wholly devoted to his art, that is, to his demonic pride and egotism, which Mons saw as corrupting, ruinous, Ich . . . Yo . . . Yorrible . . . while he continued to look at and look at himself in the fermented self-portrait of the old but immortal Rembrandt in the great exhibition at the Altes Museum in Berlin, which he was visiting for the third time that week.

# 3

# Mons's Demonstrator Samples

NE feverish night in Berlin, he decided to gather together all his real and fantastic monsters in a series of mixed works—oils, collages, drawings, etchings—that would be called *Monstruary*. His Berlin gallery owner, Double Uwe, was enthusiastic about the idea and went to his studio almost every night to urge him to get started on the project right away.

You'll be one of the monsters too—Mons warned—though I still don't know if you'll appear as the Ogre or Bluebeard.

Double Uwe burst into a cascade of uproarious laughter that shook all of his huge 150-kilo body.

Those late-autumn days in Berlin were filled with monsters. Wherever he looked—in the reflections in store windows along the Ku'damm, in the clearings and chiaroscuro of the Grunewald, in the smoke-filled air of a dingy Turkish café in Kreuzberg—he could see another monster. Sometimes all he had to do was close his eyes and the earthquake of images would begin, monstrous or barely formed faces trembling on a milky surface or at the bottom of a photographer's developing tray and then dissolving in a brilliant flash of light. I saw him draw with closed eyes a multitude of monstrous figures—grotesque, gigantic, outlandish, deformed, fantastical—on the paper tablecloth at his table in the Café Strada, which he then tore off and kept as a reminder. A few days later I saw those wine-stained sketches mixed with other, much more careful drawings of monsters and arranged around his own face on a large piece of cardboard. It was called *Demonstrator Samples.* And written in pencil, in very small letters, beneath his signature: "Painter of monsters more monstrous than monsters." He also spoke to me about the *Monstruary* project (Emil has already begun to make literature, he said, when he tested and could attest to my enthusiasm) and to certain students from the School of Fine Arts in Steinplatz, especially Klaus Holzmann, who recited some verses for him by a German Romantic proclaiming that the poet is a maker of monsters.

# 4

## On an ism

FROM the back he looks like a naked child, but in the fairly clouded mirror one can see he is a dwarf masturbating with a somewhat moronic expression of delight. And strangest of all is that the small hand holding the really large glans has bright red fingernails and is slim and feminine, in contrast to the dwarf's other hand, the right one, which is broader and rougher. Slight of hand . . .

A vestige of his childhood years, or tears? Mons, like so many other boys, had been warned at school that masturbating would stunt his growth.

And the dwarf's feminine hand? With a stumbling tongue Mons recounted, one relaxed and expansive night when he sat looking at the large lace-covered dwarf's head of the barmaid who stood on a stool behind the bar in that bar on an almost Onanien Oranienstrasse—Bárbola, he calls her—that one of his earliest memories was the vision of a reddened hand, nails painted red, caressing him in an ardently hot bath. Whose?

But the dwarf in his circular painting *Onan enano, Onan the Dwarf,* is a real model. Petit Roland. Mons met him in a stationery store on the rue des Écoles in Paris, and the exhibitionanistic dwarf posed for him several times.

# 5

# The Creature

THE smiling blond baby sitting naked in the middle of a motley assortment of flora and fauna, a tangled thicket where there fused in confusion berries, batrachians, empty eggshells, skeleton bones, entwined liana serpents, antennae, tendrils, lichens, demons' groins covered with pustules, large heads crowned with thorns, huge hideous birds, fleshy flowers, inflamed vulvas, scale-covered bellies, winged beetles, membranous wings, water worms, rags and tatters, putrescent dressings, gluttonous maws, dragons with towers and wheels, skulls with the bodies of weevils, tails of scorpions, of snakes, of worms, udders made of parchment, a toad on a withered scrotum, anuses with hemorrhoids, inflated frogs, blistered penises, phalluses with wings, fish with paws and the head of a duck, two-billed geese, plants whose leaves are riddled with eyes, bristling with beaks . . .

"You could call it *Gothic Child,*" I said when I gleefully discovered the luxuriant collage in the corner of his Kreuzberg studio. (Still punished and facing the wall, his customary treatment of doubtful works.)

"You think so?" was all Mons said, raising his arched eyebrows even further into an M. (The M of his signature . . . )

He did not think it necessary at the time to explain that the photograph of the baby had been torn out of a Nazi family magazine—found a short while before in the Nollendorfplatz flea market—that showed the perfect Aryan baby guaranteed by a progenitor chosen from the ranks of the SS and by a young, pure-blooded patriotic breeder, following the directives of the Lebensborn.

In reality the photo of the rosy baby had caught his eye because it immediately reminded him of one that a martial German collector of degenerate art and illuminated codices had framed on a kind of altar in the library of his castle near Nürnberg. And a stone's throw—as the collector informed him impassively—from the castle where Reichsmarschall Göring had spent his childhood. Marshal? Another great great art collector . . .

On the other hand—and to go on speaking of monsters and collectors—the pompous plump figure of Göring reminded him of his adoptive father—Monsieur Mons, a true mountain of flesh—and of his gallery owner Uwe Wach, "Double Uwe" to us, though you can't say this last bit in the text of the catalogue, Señor Stenographer, he said as I continued taking my notes.

# 6

## Gorgonzola

N a night of Turkish wine in Meyhane, it occurred to him to draw on a color advertisement for Gorgonzola cheese, in an illustrated magazine, the face of a nineteenth-century gentleman with a pince-nez, a goatee, and the serpentine hair of the Gorgon. Intrigued and amused, I watched him sketch the eyes, using the dark veins in the cheese.

"Who is it?"

"Another writer named Émile . . . The monster who didn't understand his friend Cézanne!"

# 7

## The Blind Eye of the Cyclops

ROM the time he began to prepare *Monstruary*, any face or body, known or unknown, could be unexpectedly monsterized. Where and when least expected. Mons attempted to fix these fleeting visions in situ, in a whoosh-swoosh of rapid strokes to capture the features. (Trolls, one might call them. Hobgoblins springing from who knows where. Phantasmal faces that sometimes formed in the dark when he closed his eyes or were abruptly superimposed on other faces he had just noticed.) And so the stocky bald man, dark glasses pushed up on his gleaming skull, who sat in the sun and sipped his beer at an open-air café on Savignyplatz and suddenly gave a great yawn, would be transformed, just a few tables away, in the notebook where Mons was noggin-doodling, into a Cyclops with an eye as large and wide-open as his mouth. But this sketch of a yawning Berliner would in a matter of seconds transport Mons light-years away to Saint-Jean-de-Luz. The great eye on the forehead, like a black plunger or an open maw, the effect produced by the diver's mask filled with mud and placed, by kids more malicious than mischievous, on the forehead of the tramp sleeping off his drunk on the beach, an empty bottle at his side. He had followed them with his eyes ever since they had found at the water's edge—at first he thought it was an octopus—the diver's mask missing its glass and had run along the beach with their prize. He would recall, looking at the boozy bum with the besmirched brow, that the terrible scene of the cannibal Cyclops whom Ulysses blinds with a sharpened red-hot stake after intoxicating him with an astute mixture of wine and wit, ended with the moralizing of a puritanically tidy professor of German origin, an abstemious vegetarian, who explicated or complicated the *Odyssey* for them: "Polyphemus lost his eye because he was drunk!" And ate meat . . .

# 8

## The Elephant Woman

THE plump, perspiring woman in the pink bikini and little white cloth hat who danced to salsa solo in the Miami Beach sun and surf, rocked by the waves of the radio playing at full volume and lying at her feet in the sand. Sitting on the beach only a few meters away, protected by his open sketchbook, Mons drew her portrait while she gracefully gyrated her weight. As she suggestively shook her ass, waist, and breasts and waved her arms like lascivious lassos and undulated her belly and opened her thighs invitingly, her nose grew inordinately longer and wider in the drawing, an elegant elephant's trunk that curled into a spiral at the tip, almost touching her right shoulder. Roundish and reddish, on paper she resembled the Indian god Ganesha.

# 9

## Zoo Illogical

HE liked zoos, and the one in Berlin—along with the one in London—was his favorite. He visited the Berlin Zoo frequently and sometimes sketched the animals—and the visitors—from life. One cold February morning, in the elephant house, he drew an old Asian elephant and then amused himself by carefully sketching at its side a louse of the same size. A short sturdy man in a loden coat, who was almost bald and had the flattened nose of a boxer, looked at the drawing and said drily before continuing on his way: *Haematomyzus elephantis.* Had he heard correctly? Walking along Budapester Strasse, soon after leaving the zoo, Mons realized that the flattened nose of the stranger in the elephant house, and his head, resembled those of a monkey . . . Mons had the ability to make the most monstrous things seem natural, the most truthful seem utterly absurd. When I saw the drawing of the monstrous louse, I could not help exclaiming: *Épouvantable!* And after hearing the anecdote of the entomological monkey, I suggested calling it *Laus Semper Pediculus.* Maldoror would like that, I added, though I did not specify if I meant the drawing or the title.

## 10

# An Insect Monster

O N E can barely see or guess at (is that a beetle-browed face under the bed?) the dun-colored silhouette of what may be an outsized head on a level with the floor behind a rose-colored veil or more probably the bedspread behind which the monstrous insect, the size of a human, is hiding. When the Swiss publisher Herz suggested to Mons that he illustrate *The Metamorphosis,* the painter immediately recalled Kafka's plea to the publisher who wanted to do an illustrated edition of the work: Above all you must not draw poor Samsa! In some way Mons respected Kafka's request, because he never did illustrate *The Metamorphosis*. An excess of reverence or a simple fear of falling into the redundant illustration?

At about this time, one feverish night, he painted in thick strokes of the brush and palette knife the unsettling oil with the German title *Was ist mit mir geschehen?*: What Has Happened to Me? (The painting memorializes a trivial experience Mons had in the Miami airport. While he was waiting for his plane, he saw an enormous cockroach start out across a wide corridor filled with hundreds of feet hurrying back and forth. The cockroach would stop abruptly when it was about to be squashed by a heavy shoe, resume the journey toward other dangerous footfalls, more trials and tribulations, come to a sudden halt, perhaps warned by a shadow or a vibration, and then prudently continue on its way. Mons began to identify with the cockroach, he said, and to agonize over the possibility that it might not succeed in crossing that river of rapid feet; the cocky cockroach kept stopping, and when the perilous foot passed, it again moved forward, until finally, happy ending, whew, it reached the promised land, a soda-dispensing machine, and scurried behind it to safety. Mons was sweating, perhaps with excitement, and it seemed to him he had won a bet. But perhaps the worst was yet to come for the cockroach. Mons said he thought then that the cockroach in Miami might wake up, after an extremely disturbing dream, transformed into a clerk in Prague.) A few nights later, after struggling with his always redoubtable doubts, he wiped away the painting as feverishly as he had painted it. But he could not free himself so easily from the insouciant insect. Impossible to fight the plague. A year later, in his house in Enfer, he once again smeared the blurred silhouette that can barely be guessed at on a level with the floor behind a fine pinkish tulle. And it seems to be opening (with its legs?) like a large M.

## II

# Oddradek

DURING the winter of 1991, Mons devoted himself to creating in his Kreuzberg studio in Berlin, with the assistance of the young Swiss sculptor Klaus Holzmann, some strange homunculimarionettes of carved sticks and strings that he presented at that year's Dokumenta in Kassel.

The critics (that anonymous monster with many tongues, not much eye, and even less head, according to Mons's expeditious definition) spoke about "neoneoconstructivism," about "purismo povero," about "Dada-long-legs" (!) and other trumped-up Tzaranean trumperies, but no one mentioned Kafka. And yet Mons did nothing more than faithfully follow the description Kafka gives of the so-called Odradek in his story "The Preoccupations of a Pater Familias":

"His appearance is that of a bobbin of thread, smooth and star-shaped, and the truth is he seems to be made of thread, but pieces of cut thread, old and knotted, a tangle of different kinds and colors. He is not merely a bobbin; from the center of the star there emerges a little transverse stick, and to this stick another is joined at a right angle. With the help of this second stick on one side and one of the arms of the star on the other, the assemblage can stand as if it had two legs.

"One would be tempted to believe that this structure once had a form adequate to its function and now is broken. But this does not seem to be the case; at least there is no such indication; nowhere can one see repairs or breaks; the assemblage appears to be useless but in its own way complete. We can say nothing more because Odradek is extraordinarily shifty and does not allow himself to be caught."

Mons had read this story by Kafka more than twenty years earlier in London and discussed it endlessly with his friends in the Artychoke group, especially the painter Albert Alter, and perhaps in order to emphasize the strangeness of this being or the strange sensation it produced in him, Mons wrote Odradek with the double D of "odd." K.'s Odradek instantly brought to mind a strange twisted root as large as a doll, with threads or little roots coming out of its dark stumps, that hung from a beam in the office of his grandfather, Dr. Verdugo. Kafka was, perhaps, an estimable excuse. But what cannot be denied is that the monsters of Mons have ancient roots.

Mons again saw or imagined his strange Oddradek hanging from a beam in his studio at Enfer, and he copied the shadow it cast—part mandrake and part hanged man—onto a canvas until he reproduced with exactitude the star or unlucky four-pointed star or enigmatic X formed by the figure as it raises its arms and spreads its legs.

## 12

# The Sponge Man

THIS series of portraits or preliminary splotches by Mons in oil and ink, completed in Enfer toward the end of 1997, depicts large soft heads with the form and texture of sponges (their pores enlarged, their eyes and mouths scarcely any bigger, though somewhat darker) multiplying in enormous rectangular multitudes crowded with spongiform heads that recall the ocean floor. When a few of them had been shown three or four years earlier in the Berlin gallery of Uwe Wach, a German art critic spoke of spongeries and sponge-men. *Schwammdrüber!* was the title of his article in the *Berliner Zeitung,* as if to say let's pass the sponge and wipe the slate clean. The sponge-man, the critic claimed, is characteristic of our time. He absorbs everything and retains nothing. He instantaneously absorbs whatever he sees and hears wherever he goes, all sorts of advertisements, discourses and concourses; televised images, virtual and vitiated; radiophonic, internetual, celltelepathic messages and newspaper headlines; and gives back everything with a huge yawn, empty and ready for use again.

Perhaps the enthusiastic critic might have been a little more cautious and less eloquent if he had even suspected Mons's method, the way he spongified. Wiped the slate clean, in fact.

In the small hours of a cold night toward the end of autumn in Berlin (after drinking like a sponge, one might properly add) Mons had enough lucidity to return to his studio to wipe away the painting he had worked on all day. At last he threw the sponge at the recently scrubbed canvas, and the mark, a new smear, made him bray his hurrays or shriek his eurekas—exactly the way it sounds—of enthusiasm. He had only to complete the sponge mark and lengthen the threads of the net so deftly woven by chance.

Months later, when they were exhibited for the first time, his sponge-men caused a good deal of ink to be spilled.

The sponge-man is avid empty man at the end of this century, every neighbor's son, you and I when we turn on the television or leaf through an illustrated magazine in a waiting room. The sponge-man, why not, is also a self-portrait of Mons. The only one he saved—it was the last one—from the series painted in Enfer.

# 13

## Mons's Mountain

N his early-afternoon walks through the Grunewald, Mons would stop at the Devil's Mountain, Teufelsberg, built with rubble from the bombing of Berlin during the war. In addition to its name, he liked the fact that it was, in a way, a construction of destruction. What geologist of pain and death could explain in detail the hidden strata, the Teutonic tectonics of its reconstructive ants? He frequently found himself at the bottom of the mountain at the same time as a stiff old man in a black overcoat who, arms folded and fist under chin, followed with an attentive eye the comings and goings of tireless children who slid down the slope and excitedly climbed back up again. Mons thought he was probably watching his grandchildren from a distance, until he noticed the hardness of his glacial gaze, the fixed eye of a bird of prey about to swoop down for the kill. Little devils! . . . he exclaimed in German beside a matron in a scarf who affectionately followed the children's games on the mountain. Mons saw himself transported to a children's costume party in Madrid, which he had reluctantly attended disguised as a red devil, red-faced from so much crying.

The strange thing is that after he noticed the old man's icy eye, he did not see him at the mountain again. His mountain? The old man's aquiline face seemed vaguely familiar. Until he finally placed him. Mons transformed him into the chimerical pensive devil who from the top of Notre Dame dominates Paris, thinks the city, perhaps. There are two versions of the painting. The first—a dark mountain or menacing beaked profile, which the young sculptor Anne Kiefer once admired, not without apprehension, in Mons's studio—was destroyed along with other works on the night of the purge, when Mons put an end to his *Monstruary*. In the recent version, executed in Enfer, the devil-gargoyle is wrapped in a black overcoat and watches at the edge of a great ravine as children tumble down the sides. The old man wears his coat collar raised, like pointed ears, and the mountain down below and in the distance seems like his own shadow.

# 14

# The Monster of Mons

Mons's fondness for savage events and circumstances. One afternoon a few years ago, on a summer visit to Enfer, he drove me in his old London taxi to Gambais, some forty kilometers away, on the pretext of visiting the cemetery where the Cubist painter Robert Delaunay lies buried. Delaunay? I was surprised, not suspecting that kind of veneration . . . Until we reached a wall in Gambais (not the one around the cemetery) and an ordinary tree-shaded house; I recognized the mosaic rhombuses on the cornices, for they also adorned the corners of his triptych *Bluebeard's Secret*, which depicts Landru dressed as a magician (his bald head and pointed beard also recall Mons) who performs his acts of prestidigitation at a small iron stove, watched over by the portraits of various women on the wall. He had taken me to Gambais so that I could see the house where Landru made the unfortunate women he seduced (nine?) disappear. Who would dare call him undesirable? Henry the Desired! Mons choked with laughter. Don't tell me his name wasn't fabulous: Henri-Désiré . . . Mons loping through the wasteland of Landru.

In the spring of 1997, as reports multiplied regarding the butcher of the Belgian city of Mons, who scattered pieces of women (three, five, or more women murdered?) wrapped in garbage bags in places with significant names—the River of Hate, the Road of Disquiet, the Road of Solitude—Mons would telephone me from different cities and comment excitedly about the discoveries. But I'm not the monster of Mons . . . he would joke. The fact is, he never set foot in Mons. On several occasions he had been ready to visit that ancient city in southwestern Belgium, almost on the French border, between the rivers Trouille (Fear) and Haine (Hate), but a dream kept him from going near it. He too felt fear or *trouille* . . . In that long-ago dream, which he believed pre-monitory, he was driving a black car (his English taxi?) and suddenly lost control, and before he crashed he caught sight of the sign that said MONS in black letters. He knew almost everything about the city of Mons and its nearby depressed industrial zones, its convent school Saint Wandru, its Gothic city hall, its railroad station and adjacent narrow streets, the prison where Verlaine was confined, but he could not approach the city—forbidden—of his name. Perhaps the picture recently painted in Enfer, *Le Monstre reprit ses chemins*, in which one sees the dark silhouette of Mons holding black garbage bags in his hands and walking toward a gloomy horizon where the outline of the school and several chimneys stand out, was his way of approaching the city in his dream. But the stones on the ground are, or seem to be, the heads of women. I believe beyond the shadow of a doubt that I recognize the pale, staring head of Eva Lalka peering out through the weeds.

# 15

# The Venus in the Rearview Mirror

THE Venus of the Mirror gave him the pose (though forced to twist around, naked on what seems to be the seat in a utility vehicle, she too shows us her back) and, in passing, the curves of her waist, hips and buttocks, somewhat more athletic than those of the only nude painted by Velázquez.

I saw her taking shape this past August in the violet space of the canvas placed, in the studio in Enfer, across from the violet backseat of a Renault Twingo, which Mons had found in an auto salvage yard that announced itself at the side of the road, near Avernes, in large white letters: FER HARRY. Whenever we passed by in Mons's taxi, we celebrated the sign.

A suspicious dark brown stain (blood?) on the upholstery.

Could the model—the real Venus—have posed on that seat from a Twingo?

In the painting the seat is enveloped in an aura of violets and light purples, perhaps in a field on a summer night. She is the light that illuminates the night.

Because her back is turned, one can hardly see the gentle oval of her face, framed by a dazzling mane of albino hair. As Mons painted her from head to toe, lingering especially over her purple nails, I paid attention to the barely sketched rearview mirror, where, I supposed, the face of the Venus of the Twingo would finally be reflected. I knew she was in the life and that Mons had recently met her. In fact, for some time he saw her only fleetingly, in the distance. When Mons returned to Enfer at nightfall from pictorial hunting expeditions in his English taxi, he would see her parked in a violet Twingo at the side of the road, particularly at the entrance to a bridge over the Seine, in Gargenville. A beacon in the night to attract her prey. The Twingo, its interior brightly lit, a fluorescent wig gleaming like a decoy. At night, at the entrance to the bridge over the Seine, a line of trucks parked next to a hotel-restaurant. Sometimes Mons noticed the Twingo, its lights turned off, parked a little farther away on a path in the fields. The laborer of love, he used to call her. One night when he saw the glowing wig inside the Twingo, he decided to satisfy his curiosity. Mons, at heart, is more Actaeon than actor. Like Actaeon, he wanted only to look. That's what he said. He wanted to look at her up close, see her face. Only her face? He parked beside the Twingo and struck up a conversation. And they immediately struck a deal. She, both suspicious and flattered, accepted his proposition. To let him sketch her there, in her wig, in the lighted car. A phantasmagorical scene on the bridge. Mons resting his sketchbook on the hood of his antiquated taxi, across from the firefly of love. Did he see her only that night? Mons does not always answer the questions of his eminent biographer. As his brush strokes continued to reveal that well-muscled, naked body, I waited to see her face suddenly appear. What was she like? If I told you, you wouldn't believe me. She really wore the wig so as not to be recognized. During the day she worked in a nearby post office. Sitting on the Twingo seat, facing Mons's Venus, I recalled the times so long ago when I would settle on the settee in the National Gallery in London in front of Velázquez's Venus and try to see more clearly the rather blurred and indistinct face of the beauty in the mirror. And I remember Mons's comment in situ: Her ass is cleaner than her face! I spent several nights toward the end of August near the bridge over the Seine, in the taxi driven so dangerously by Mons—a left-handed driver with a right-handed wheel—but we did not see the violet Twingo of the pieceworker of love. Did he need to see her again to go on painting her? On that August afternoon it occurred to him to visit the Venus de Milo, and I accompanied him to the Louvre, swarming with tourists. He forgot about the Venus with the million or more admirers and walked around the less-hemmed-in Hermaphrodite dozing on the divan, and even made some sketches of a half-moon buttock and the marmoreal sleeping member. We spent more nights near the bridge. The line of trucks still parked for the night in the same place, but not a sign of the phantom Twingo. The wig gleamed only in the studio at Enfer. As he prepared to put the final touches on his violet painting, Mons handed me a page of a local newspaper. Another sad, sadistic crime story. Her name was Dominique. Also called Lady Twingo. Large, heavily made-up eyes in a long, bony face. There was also a photograph of the Twingo in which she practiced prostitution. Practice, what a word. And the police were broadening their investigation to include certain truck drivers from eastern countries who might have had relations with the transvestite Dominique Couto because the weapon used in the crime was a hammer of Czech manufacture, with which her skull and face had been beaten in and completely disfigured. Mons did not reflect in the rearview mirror of his painting the mysterious face of his Venus, but he did reproduce with absolute fidelity and perfection the genitals of the Hermaphrodite in the Louvre. If Venus supplied the buttocks, Mercury provided the quicksilver prick, I might have said, but Mons would have misinterpreted this as mere inopportune wordplay. I look at the cock in the rearview mirror, and it seems to me that more than anything else Mons wanted to give the painting a touch of tenderness.

# 16

## The Diva Bottle

THE series of drawings, generally in small format, depicting artists and writers who were fond of drink: Hals, Soutine, Munch, Poe, Joyce, Faulkner, Lowry . . . The most terrible, perhaps, *Muse and Musician:* Mussorgsky, black hair unruly and a reddish beard spilling over his chest, contemplates with bloodshot eyes, in the firelight, a whitish bottle that seems to float in air.

Another no less surprising and sanguine apparition: the head of a red-haired woman emerges, revealing her body as far as her red pubis, from the neck of a half-empty bottle of red wine. The rest of her naked body also appears red in the semitransparent bottle. Her breasts, full and round, are aureoled in red and the nipples blaze like live coals, as vivid as her eyes and partially opened lips.

The nude and the bottle seem to come from the world of Magritte, the fiery head perhaps from the spectral world of Munch, but I was sure the brilliant idea for the painting was really inspired by the story "The Princess Brambilla" by

Hoffmann. Better call her Bombilla—the lightbulb—Mons protested, and he assured me he had never heard of any such story. For my part, I had never heard, until that afternoon in Enfer, of the woman he calls the Mute Marquise and the Mistress of Silence. And, playing with her name, Silvia Silente. An Italian marquise who breeds horses on an estate— with an eighteenth-century white manor house—not far from Enfer. One of the few neighbors with whom Mons has any relationship. Some years ago, when she learned that a well-known painter was living in the area, she sent him a letter asking if he would be interested in painting portraits of her best thoroughbreds. An amused Mons responded that he did not paint horses without Amazons, but in order not to offend her said he was willing to visit her stables. She sent him a rather formal invitation, and, with the wink of an accomplice, received him at the entrance to her neoclassical house dressed as an Amazon. A redhead of great presence and fine lines in her close-fitting black velvet hunting jacket. Until then Mons had not known she was a deaf-mute, but, he claims, they can speak for hours with their eyes. And not only their eyes. I don't know if it was on the first visit that they established the ritual of the *diva botella*. They sit facing one another across a large table, in the light of candelabra, and with a bottle of good Bordeaux (always Bordeaux) between them, they begin the mute dialogue and the silent decanting of the wine. She writes something to Mons on a tablet, trademark STENO, passes it to him, and Mons responds on the next page, sometimes only with a sketch. In this way they dialogue deliberately, dispatching the bottle and the tablet, glass by glass and sentence by sentence. They begin another bottle and another notebook, until pen and hand fail them. She has suffered a good deal in her sixty years: condemned to silence since childhood, years of marriage to a dishonest fortune hunter who died not long ago of cancer, above all because of the death of her son, thrown against a tree by a horse shortly before she met Mons, and the coldheartedness of her daughter, who lives in Boston and never deigns to visit her or invite her for a visit. Instead of horses Mons began to draw drunkards for her. Hals, Soutine, Munch, Pollock . . . aureoled in a red Mons calls Rothschild *"rouge,"* and besotted would also become those inflamed faces that illuminate the nights with his silent friend. Modigliani, Gorky, Grosz . . . the entire series for her, his true diva, as they exchange confidences in the dim candlelight. *In vino veritas,* all the truths of the heart and soul that the mouth cannot say. And he also painted a horse for her, on a bottle standing empty on the edge of Edmonde's Rothko-red tub. And told her, perhaps, as he told me one night when he was half-drunk in Enfer, that he was the one who had driven her, Edmonde, to drink and really drowned her in alcohol. And that Edmonde opened her veins not only with a razor but with a broken glass as well. The spirit of wine ignites, perhaps, in the neck of the bottle where the beautiful red head of the diva truth emerges naked.

## 17

# Polyptych of the Hanged Man
## (Le Bal du pendule)

T HE long white patches of paint peeling from an
outside wall of the house-studio in Enfer, next to
the entrance gate to the courtyard, on the chemin
d'Avernes, look like the silhouettes of flamenco dancers
who pirouette and raise their arms and bend their legs in the
most varied postures, as Mons pointed out to me when he
had already used them in the six paintings of his polyptych
*Le Bal du pendule*. The pendant straw-figure hanged man
dangles from a beam, in a different position on each panel,
surrounded by the strange white dancers, most prominent
among them the androgynous figure with red breasts and
black legs. The silhouette of Edmonde the dancer? Or perhaps Edmonde is the graceful arabesque or white figure in
the first painting of the polyptych, who stands on one leg
and raises the other and lifts her arms beneath the hanged
man hanging as rigid as a sword of Damocles.

It is a danse macabre of phantoms in which one can
also recognize the characteristic silhouettes (each in its own
painting and in a different position, designated or pointed
out among all the other dancers by the dangling hanged
man) of Mons's other dead: Anne Kiefer, Helen Gulick, Eva
Lalka, Professor Reck, Ziegel the architect . . .

There is also a small rigid black figure like a half-burned
log next to the great fireplace in the first painting, who

is Madame Pierret, the neighboring farmwife who keeps house for him and tells Mons a thousand and one stories about the village. Mons also calls her the Daughter of Lightning because a roguish bolt of lightning came down the chimney in her kitchen, embraced her as if they were doing the waltz, and took only her slipper before escaping to the countryside, shooting off sparks. . . . That is why, Mons claims, she is so dark.

Mons knew that his studio, which occupies the entire first floor of the house, had once been the village dance hall. But Madame Pierret told him that long before that, during the war, it had been the farm where poor Gervais hung himself. Perhaps that was why Mons decided to add to the polyptych a self-portrait with the large, arrogant head of a Cyclops in whose wide-open eye there is reflected a beam that projects like a diving board. What did he mean to say? I was uneasy. Behold, a beam is in thine own eye, was his almost evangelical reply.

# II

# Mons in Enfer

COME to Hell! is Mons's habitual joke. A really infernal cold. I saw again the white patches dancing on the gray wall next to the dark red door. I went to Enfer because he asked me to come. Right away. He knew I was traveling and followed my route with his repeated urgent message. I picked up Mons's message only three days later, when I returned to the Hotel Majestic in Barcelona. As always, he could have told me again, you've come too late. In the paved part of the courtyard all the half-blackened paintings. Almost like Madame Pierret, in her dark raincoat and high rubber boots, who stood beside me and contemplated the mound. At the foot of the outside staircase, evergreen with verdigris. One would say he was in a hurry to burn them, piling them so close to the house, or else he didn't want to muddy his feet in the middle of the courtyard. The scorched smell still hovered. Madame Pierret had not dared to clean the courtyard or the studio until Monsieur Mons returned. Ashes, char, fragments of colors . . .

There remained, in derisive witness, the scribblings I had written for the pictures at an exhibition that should have been titled "Pictures for the Fire of Enfer," just a few pages among jars of paint and dirty rags in battle disarray on the large table in the studio that had once been a dance hall, let the danse macabre continue, and before that the farm of a hanged man, and the poor devil who hung himself from the high beam long before Mons's first wife followed his example by other means, perhaps inspired in Mons his black thoughts and blacker paintings. On the wall, over the door to the studio, written (a new inscription) in large black letters in French: *En Enfer, il n'y a pas de Rédemption.* His angular handwriting . . . Is there no redemption in Enfer? And yet he seemed to be working so animatedly just a few days before. In the courtyard his old taxi still loaded down with the canvases he planned to paint on future excursions. First to Auvers-sur-Oise to paint a shadow of van Gogh. And then to the bend of the Seine in Vétheuil, near the white house high on the cliff that he calls the Portuguese house, to paint a white and gray debacle, several blocks of ice downriver, one of them recognizable as a pale dead face . . . In spite of the rain he drove me in his funereal English car to Edmonde's corner, he said, a few months ago, before he showed me the sketch. Frozen Ophelia . . . I suggested the title without understanding his intentions. The sphinx of the ice . . .

Again I admired from his studio window the silver bars on gray—the row of birches against the sky—that Mons incorporated as minimalist barred windows in those malicious works entitled *Suprematisse I, II, III* . . . I preferred to see that distant painting than the ruin at my feet.

*Mons Veneris* did not meet its end burning in the courtyard—too difficult to transport—but Mons ripped off its skin and tore it to shreds. On the floor of the studio I could recognize the fragment of black stocking that had belonged to Ara, Mons's stepsister, the gentle object of his early masturbation in Madrid. (Unless it was the stocking-snake of Mélusine's striptease.) And Anne Kiefer's little clay belly. And the leap in bed that marks the luminous volumes of Helen Gulick. And the smooth rump of Eva Lalka riding her ebony lover. And the apple-breasts of the hooded woman. And a good portion of her slender legs sheathed in black stockings. And her pubis painted by an intrepid Mons. On countless nights she would ride him in her hood, and when the awful bilious face on her belly was about to crush the painter's face, he unfailingly woke up.

In the studio there were five canvases of five bellies (the same one?) with punctures or burns in the middle that outlined on the wall the hollow silhouette of the same face. The letters V.I.T.R.I.O.L. burned into one belly beneath the empty face. Or fetus? Mons the Ripper . . . Vitriolic Victor . . .

In an old-fashioned spa in Baden-Baden, where his mother had been recuperating a few months earlier from her attacks of arthritis, Mons discovered the perfect profile of a Gothic Virgin in another octogenarian who was having her breakfast alone at a nearby table. A short while later, when she walked past them, she showed the other side of her face, which was horribly burned. She said that in her youth a jealous rival had thrown vitriol at her. The greater horror was the error: the jealous—and confused—woman had mistaken her for the rival she wanted to disfigure.

I don't know if Mons ever drew the burned side of her face or affliction, or incorporated it into his *Têtes brûlées*. From Baden-Baden he sent me a drawing of the stag or Actaeon leaping at the entrance to the spa on Hirschstrasse.

I tried in vain to decipher the burned acronym. Visage Inside The Ruined Illusion . . . Had Mons found the true face of his patron with the twisted tusks? Or his unattainable self-portrait? He tried again to paint the portrait of the man he calls Sir Boar. Curiously enough, and I'll have to tell him about it with dictionary in hand, in a sense he is Mons. Boar, *jabalí* in Spanish, comes from an Arabic word, *yábal,* that means "mountain." Courage! It amounts to the same thing . . .

On a recent trip to Colmar for another viewing of Isenheim's inexhaustible retable of his god and supreme creator Grünewald, Mons had an encounter, perhaps not fortuitous, he said, in the Unterlinden Museum, with an elegant German woman, Eva Eberhardt, still youthful in appearance and very attractive, who had been widowed a few years earlier and who knew a great deal about Gothic painting. She had approached Mons to watch him sketch on an envelope the superposed feet of Grünewald's crucified Christ on which he had included like a wound the diagrammatic image of another crucifixion. And demonstrated that she knew by heart even the tiniest sore and pustule and stigmata of Grünewald's creatures. They continued the conversation in a nearby café inevitably named Chez Hansi, and then they went to visit the picturesque corners of La Petite Venise. The flutter of their black coats . . . To be incorporated into his next black painting? Mons also told me on the phone that his German Eva had lived, in the late sixties, in Little Venice. They had probably crossed paths more than once in London's Venezuela. After that they went to Strasbourg by the wine route, in her Mercedarian white Mercedes. They did not have time to visit the cathedral but strolled past the Christmas stands that surrounded it. They ate supper in the Kammerzell and ended up sleeping together in the heights and narrows of a tiny attic room in the old building. Mons admitted that he drank without moderation the Riesling that had caused so much laughter in his friend the critic Joyce Adam, may she rest in peace, and that the new Eva never turned down a toast. Each *Prosit* brought them into closer proximity. Vivaciously she shook out the blond hair that framed the animated oval of her face, somewhat flushed by now, with that charming cleft in her chin. (His obsession with dimples . . . Could it have been an illusion?) They staggered up to their seventh heaven. When Eva began to undress, with Mons's help, there in the shadow of the cathedral, he asked her not to take off her black stockings yet because her pale slender body, the albino spume of her mound of Venus, and the intense sea smell of her cunt, reminded him of the hooded woman in the hotel at Charing Cross. Had he already told her the story of the portrait on her belly, or did that come later? And she allowed herself to be cajoled and cowled, laughing, with her own black scarf. Or was it his? Mons would swear—but he drank too much Riesling and Gewürztraminer—that the sallow face once again pressed against his, trying to sink its tusks into him when she spurred him on, galloping toward the garden of delight and torture as she dug sharp nails into his wrists and pressed his hands against the headboard. Ecce Pictor. Or Victor? Pictor Mons. As one of his artist-painter stamps said half in jest. They had spoken before—or was it afterward—about the lost secret of the old masters.

Mmm! Memling himself could not have loved me better, she said the next morning before she said good-bye, because she had to get back to Fribourg early. Was she a professor of art? Mons thinks so. Though she probably taught in Heidelberg. And Eva Eberhardt (Dr. Eva Eberhardt?), to prove to

him that she really was well informed and could track down allusions, mentioned Memling again and recommended to Mons that he be sure to visit the Musée des Beaux-Arts before he went back to Paris.

I read again the words scrawled by Mons on the brochure of the Musée des Beaux-Arts in Strasbourg, there on the table in his studio, next to my text about his most recent works, and all those old records he tirelessly listened to over and over again when he painted them: *Pictures at an Exhibition, Lulu,* Gesualdo's *Madrigals,* Handel's *Cantata Spagnuola (No se enmendará jamás),* and—as he calls them—the *Gouldberg Variations* . . .

"Memling the first?" he wrote on the brochure. And then: "She too is incubating in her glass cube."

Her glass cube . . . At first I thought he was referring to his *dame* on the Ku'damm.

I still try to imagine Mons's astonished face in the museum in Strasbourg, which perhaps was reflected in the glass cube in the center of the small room, as he scrutinized the image the size of an illumination in a breviary. His astonished face seeing itself reflected in the small panel on the right, *Diable en Enfer,* of Memling's *Triptych of Earthly Vanity and Heavenly Redemption.*

Perhaps he looked first at the central panel of the triptych, where the naked beauty in sandals, a diadem in her long blond hair, allows herself to be doubly admired in the mirror she holds in her right hand, conscious that the focus of everyone's gaze is her mound of Venus with its open cleft. Did it remind him of the pubis of the hooded woman?

Another private part, with toad, would probably draw his

attention to the shriveled mummy and skull on the left panel of the triptych.

I imagine Mons walking around the glass cube to see the triptych from the other side. The coat of arms with the motto he could also apply to himself: *Nul bien sans peine.* Each work has its cost . . . The Lord surrounded by four musician angels. The skull (with teeth like bullets . . . ) in a niche.

And again, still astonished, standing in front of the Devil in Hell.

Would Mons's strange anonymous patron have wanted to copy that painting by Memling from life?

Perhaps he really did resemble the tusked and terrible face (Sir Boar? Or is his name Legion?) on the abdomen of the androgynous devil with the helix ears, divided beard (the cleft of Satan?), little red tits like poisoned apples, and black paws about to prance recklessly down into the jaws of Hell; or perhaps Mons saw that minuscule image by Memling long ago, and it was etched more or less unconsciously in his mind only to be superimposed on the image of his London patron and to reappear in his own nightmares, caprices, and monstruaries. Most terrible of all is that it resembles him.

Does one come to resemble what one most admires, loves, or even fears? I leave the question hanging. With many other doubts and conjectures.

Mons hurried back to Enfer to complete the destruction. Why did he call me? Probably so I could be a witness to his new sudden flight. He did what he had so often done: he played airport roulette. He arrives dragging his suitcase, looks at an announcement of departures, Vienna, Zurich, Amsterdam, and the first name that appears is his next destination. I've just spoken on the phone with Double Uwe, as accustomed as I to Mons's impetuous departures, and he tells me not to worry. Mons is fine. And nearby, this time. In Madrid. Double Uwe is flying tomorrow to Madrid to see for himself. And spend Saint Sylvester's night with him. Or is it Walpurgisnacht? Mons told him he doesn't leave the Prado because he has a great mountain of ideas for resuming (won't he ever change?) his *Monstruary*.

A NOTE ON THE TYPE

THIS BOOK was set in Monotype Dante, a typeface designed by Giovanni Mardersteig (1892–1977). Conceived as a private type for the Officina Bodoni in Verona, Italy, Dante was originally cut only for hand composition by Charles Malin, the famous Parisian punch cutter, between 1946 and 1952. Its first use was in an edition of Boccaccio's *Trattatello in laude di Dante* that appeared in 1954. The Monotype Corporation's version of Dante followed in 1957. Although modeled on the Aldine type used for Pietro Cardinal Bembo's treatise *De Aetna* in 1495, Dante is a thoroughly modern interpretation of the venerable face.

Composed by Creative Graphics,
Allentown, Pennsylvania
Printed and bound by R. R. Donnelley,
Harrisonburg, Virginia
Designed by Virginia Tan